"You have a lot to offer the boys.

"You have skill with your hands. You have patience in working with them. They'd really benefit from having a man spend some time with them." Laureen paused and gathered her breath for her sell job. "I was wondering if you'd consider taking on a project with them. Maybe teach them some simple woodworking skills. Or—" At the look on Pete's face, she broke off.

"You must be kidding. I have no desire to be part of your absolution. Besides, I'm too busy."

Laureen jerked to her feet. "Absolution? Is that what you think this is? Is that how you see my work? Selfish vainglory? You think I'm suffering from a guilt complex? Well, you couldn't be more wrong." She pulled herself tall and straight. "And we'll get along fine without any help from you."

LINDA FORD draws on her own experiences living in the Canadian prairie and Rockies to paint wonderful adventures in romance and faith. She lives in Alberta, Canada, with her family, writing as much as her full-time job of taking care of a paraplegic and four kids who are still at home will allow. Linda says, "I thank God that He has given me a full productive life and that I'm not bored. I thank Him for placing a little bit of the creative energy revealed in His creation into me, and I pray I might use my writing for His honor and glory."

Books by Linda Ford

HEARTSONG PRESENTS

Don't miss out on any of our super romances. Write to us at the following address for information on our newest releases and club information.

Heartsong Presents Readers' Service
PO Box 719
Uhrichsville, OH 44683

Or visit www.heartsongpresents.com

Forever in My Heart

Linda Ford

Heartsong Presents

This story is dedicated to those people who have hearts like Laureen's—big enough to love children not born to them—and a faith like Pete discovered, enabling them to bring these children into their homes and make them part of their family.

To adoptive and foster parents: May God bless and strengthen you.

A note from the Author:
I love to hear from my readers! You may correspond with me by writing:

Linda Ford
Author Relations
PO Box 719
Uhrichsville, OH 44683

ISBN 1-59310-248-8

FOREVER IN MY HEART

Our mission is to publish and distribute inspirational products offering exceptional value and biblical encouragement to the masses.

Scripture taken from the HOLY BIBLE, NEW INTERNATIONAL VERSION®. NIV®. Copyright © 1973, 1978, 1984 by International Bible Society. Used by permission of Zondervan Publishing House. All rights reserved.

All of the characters and events in this book are fictitious. Any resemblance to actual persons, living or dead, or to actual events is purely coincidental.

PRINTED IN THE U.S.A.

Or check out our Web site at www.heartsongpresents.com

one

"There's good news, and there's bad news."

Laureen Baker knew it was unrealistic to think all the news would be good. During her three-week holiday, something was bound to have gone wrong, if not with the kids or the relatives, then certainly with the hot-water tank. Laureen hated to borrow trouble, but she might as well have all the facts. She glanced around the bedroom-turned-office, her eyes narrowing as if she'd discover in the numerous photos and children's drawings hung on the wall hidden messages to reveal the happenings of the past three weeks.

"Give me the good news first," she said.

Marj Carnes, her capable assistant who had been giving the report, looked up. "We have a new neighbor."

What did that crooked grin of Marj's mean? "A friendly grandma figure, I hope."

Marj grimaced. "He's male and not the least bit friendly. The bad news is we've been warned to keep the kids out of his territory. And his yard is full of enticements—tools, lumber, all sorts of things to make little boys want to take a look."

"Great." Laureen glanced toward the door. "Speaking of which—where are the boys?" Her anxiety mounting, she hurried down the hall and out to the lawn.

The warm sun and sparkling sky did nothing to ease her tension. The worn lawn, one corner piled high with toys, was empty and quiet. Her first day back and already—

"Michael! Davey!" she called. "Kyler? Where are you?"

The silence echoed around her; then a scuffling sound drew her gaze to the fence separating them from their neighbor. One board leaned crookedly. She hurried to the scraggly tree huddled against the edge of the yard and saw behind it the gap in the fence. Just big enough to allow the boys to escape.

"Great," she muttered. "Just great." The previous neighbors had been an older couple who both worked during the day. They'd been tolerant of the noise and occasional intrusion of the boys who lived at the Barnabas Christian Home, affectionately known as the Barney House. But now they had a grumpy old man next door who, according to Marj, had made it understood he wouldn't be quite so accommodating.

She stood on tiptoe to peer across the fence, but all she saw was the cement-pad patio, an umbrella-sheltered table, two green lawn chairs, and an uncluttered yard.

No little boys.

She looked toward the back gate in their yard, then gave another long considering look at the hole in the fence. Why not? It would be quicker than going around, and it wasn't as if she'd be setting a bad example.

Yeah, she thought, already knowing what route she would choose.

Pushing aside the leafy branches of the stunted maple tree and leaning the board farther out of place to make room for her wider body, she dropped to her knees and wormed her way through the narrow opening.

Her legs still in her own yard, her head and shoulders trespassing in the next, she glanced around and caught the flash of a yellow T-shirt and blue denim shorts ducking around the corner of the garage.

"Boys," she hissed. "Get back here."

She heard shuffling and Michael telling someone to be quiet.

"You're going to get us all into a pile of trouble," she whispered harshly, hoping they would hear and choose to help her out.

Nothing. Even the whispering and shuffling stopped. Ominous quiet. What were they up to? No good, she could guarantee. If she hoped to maintain peace with the new neighbor she better get them back ASAP. That left her with no choice but to go get them and march them home.

She eased her arms forward and pulled. And came to a sharp halt as her hip bones ground into the boards. She wriggled and grunted, but she was stuck in a boy-width opening that was inches too narrow for a grown-up-sized body. She flipped to her side to make herself narrower. Keeping her head down and closing her eyes, she groaned and wormed forward, her attention focused on working her lower half through the fence.

Safely through, she lay there for a moment, catching her breath. At least her undignified passage had not been witnessed.

She opened her eyes and saw a pair of boots, inches from her nose. A gasp steamed across her teeth. She closed her eyes. *Please, God, let this be my imagination.* But when she peeked through her eyelashes, they were still there. Dark brown work boots. Scuffed and stained with black. Steel-toed and hard enough looking to be real.

Now would be a good time for the ground to open up and swallow her.

Certain she looked like a beached whale wallowing on the

lawn, she swallowed hard and edged backward, praying she could slide back through the opening with more ease and grace than she had coming forward.

"You might as well get up," a deep, annoyed voice said.

Laureen took a long breath and lifted her head. Slowly she dragged her gaze upward. From her awkward viewpoint the legs seemed very long. The crossed forearms proclaimed annoyance. She registered the muscled shoulders. Their set didn't look welcoming, either.

By the time she could see his face, her neck muscles were stretched like a curious owl and her cheeks burned. She hadn't felt so conspicuously awkward since grade seven when she'd fallen flat on her face crossing the stage before an auditorium full of people.

What happened to the old man who lives here? she wondered wildly.

This man was young and strong and. . . She tried to swallow, but her clumsy position made it impossible so she settled for a grimace.

He had dark brown eyes that stared boldly—challengingly. A hint of gold caught along the edges of his brown hair backlit by warm sunshine. Deep creases lined his cheeks. She felt certain they would deepen into beguiling grooves when he smiled.

Which he wasn't likely to do given the invasion of his yard by three little boys and a scuttled whale.

Laureen scooted to her knees, then scrambled to her feet. She dusted her jeans and smoothed her hair and concentrated on wiping a few blades of grass from her elbow. Anything for an excuse to avoid looking at the man.

Even though he stood motionless and quiet, his stance and unmoving body shouted annoyance.

She tried not to cringe as she faced him. No point in letting him know how ungraceful and embarrassed she felt. She met his dark, steady look and felt exposed. The feeling deepened as his expression remained impassive, his lips set in a so-let's-hear-your-excuse line.

Laureen scrubbed her palms against her sides and bit the corner of her mouth. "I–I—" She clamped her teeth together then tried again. "You—"

The man's expression was anything but welcoming. If only he would say something. Like maybe "How nice to meet you." Or "That was quite a feat, crawling through that tiny opening in the fence." But, no, he regarded her as if he'd found a snake in his grass.

"It was quicker—" She waved toward the hole in the fence. "I wanted—"

What had she wanted? She couldn't remember. Oh, yes, Michael, Davey, and Kyler.

"The boys—" She glanced past him. Where were they? Sanity returned. "I'm sorry. When I saw the boys had gone through the hole, I thought—" What did it matter that she'd hoped to avoid annoying the new neighbor? It was quite apparent she'd failed.

Forcing aside her discomfort, she introduced herself. "Laureen Baker, supervisor of the Barnabas Home. How do you do?" She held out her hand, half expecting him to ignore it, but he slowly uncurled his arms and grasped her hand. She was alarmed to note her fingers trembled. His hand was warm and firm—the hand of a working man. As if she needed to shake hands with him to know that. From his boots to the width of his shoulders—trademarks of a man familiar with physical labor—he reeked of strength and power.

"Pete Long," he said. Again that slow, lazy, deep voice. She could almost feel it vibrating in her chest. She'd always been a sucker for a deep, melodious voice. "I think that's what you're looking for."

She jerked around to follow the direction of his nod.

Three boys stood side by side, looking deceptively innocent.

"Boys, you know you aren't allowed over here."

Michael, the oldest at seven, held out a red-and-blue-striped ball. "We had to get our ball."

She nodded. Whether it had landed in the yard accidentally or not was beside the point. "Next time come and tell me first. That way we can get Mr. Long's permission. Now let's go home and leave the man alone." Hurrying toward the boys, she touched them on the shoulders and gently turned them about.

A voice rumbled behind her. "Try using the gate this time."

"Of course," she muttered, embarrassment burning the tips of her ears. As if she made a habit of crawling through fences. At the gate she paused and glanced over her shoulder. "Sorry for the intrusion. It won't happen again." She chose to look at the fence rather than meet his gaze again.

"I hope not. This place is off-limits."

She gritted her teeth. He might as well have uttered a dare to the boys. Knowing something was forbidden only made it more enticing. It would keep her on her toes to make sure they stayed safely in their own yard.

She let her breath out slowly and pulled her emotions under control. It didn't pay to let things get under her skin. That only served to make her less effective in dealing with the kids. After all, it wasn't their fault she'd been caught in such an awkward position.

She marched the boys down the alley, into their own backyard, and up the steps into the house.

She lined them up and leaned over to face them on their own level. "Boys," she began, "Mr. Long does not want you in his yard. It's dangerous over there. Understand?"

Michael nodded, his expression rebellious.

His brother, six-year-old Davey, gave her an innocent look she knew all too well could be very deceiving.

And Kyler, almost six, his curly light brown hair and blue eyes such a contrast to the darkness of the other two, met her gaze with wide-eyed silence.

She sighed and ruffled his hair. What went on in that little head? Kyler hadn't said a word in two years. Not since the authorities had found him crouched beside the body of his mother. Another fatal overdose from a batch of crack packing an unusually large wallop.

She straightened. "Go on out and play."

As they raced outside, she watched them thoughtfully. She had her task set out before her with these three.

Michael and Davey had been in the home three months. Their lives had been a series of moves as their mother went from relationship to relationship, sometimes taking the boys, sometimes leaving them with friends or relatives. They'd been in and out of foster care, often separated from each other as well as from their mother. Small wonder they acted out. Since their arrival at the Barney House, there had been significant improvement in their behavior, although Michael still had an anger problem while Davey chose to retreat behind a blank stare.

The administrators of the home had tried in vain to locate their mother. Until they did it was a matter of wait-and-see until the future could be decided for the pair.

It was a situation Laureen found herself impatient with. Her goal was always to see these kids helped with their problems and placed permanently as soon as possible. Her fervent prayer was God would aid them in locating the boys' mother so permanency plans could be made.

Kyler, on the other hand, had been with them almost since he'd been found. In that time he'd had extensive counseling and was the recipient of much prayer. A young couple, cousins of his mother, had agreed to adopt him when he was ready. They wanted to see him talking before they took him home. The staff, for the most part, agreed.

Laureen sighed. Part of her agreed; she longed for the day he would open up to them. But part of her wondered if it wasn't Kyler's defense against further pain. He was smart enough to know the home wasn't permanent. Maybe not talking was his way of letting them know he didn't want to get attached to someone only to have them taken from his life.

For a few minutes she watched the boys play. Kyler had retreated to the sandbox in the corner with a heap of little cars and trucks. Patiently he pushed them back and forth in the sand. The other two were chasing the red and blue ball back and forth across the yard.

They paused close to Pete Long's fence and studied it. *Don't do it*, she warned silently. They glanced toward the house, saw her watching, and resumed playing.

Forbidden territory, she thought, *seems all the more appealing*. If only Pete Long hadn't unknowingly uttered a challenge.

She tapped her chin. Too bad he hadn't been a little more welcoming. It would have taken away the allure.

She thought again of those strong hands, the dark eyes.

What would he look like if he smiled? She pictured deep creases in his cheeks.

Suddenly she realized she was as bad as the boys, wondering about forbidden territory. She had no intention of letting anything deflect her from her purpose of seeing these boys, and the ones who would follow, given a chance at life.

"No more of this," she muttered, pushing away from the window. She didn't need any complications in her life or any distractions from her work.

❧

"All done?" Marj asked as Laureen left the office a couple hours later.

Laureen straightened from locking the door behind her and brushed her brow with an exaggerated sweep of her arm. "Is the paperwork ever done? Hey, those cookies smell good."

Marj scooped several hot cookies off the baking sheet to a plate. "Marj's famous chocolate chip cookies. Sit down. I'll get us some coffee."

"Just what I need—the coffee, not the cookies." She eyed the steaming cookies. " 'Course I could use some chocolate, too. Good for what ails me."

"And that would be?"

Laureen shrugged. "Just a figure of speech. Actually, I'm glad to be back. I missed the boys."

"I wondered if you'd come in before you were due back. But not even a phone call." Marj laughed. "I'm impressed."

"Hey. I was on holiday." She wasn't about to give Marj a chance to gloat by admitting how often she'd reached for the phone to check on things at the home. She studied her coworker. Plump and homey looking—it was Marj who provided the mother figure in the place.

"So you really got a chance to relax?"

Laureen stretched like a cat waking from a long nap. "After a week of helping my parents clean their garage and attic, I spent the rest of my holiday at the lake. My brothers and their families were there for most of a week; and then I had the rest of the time to do nothing but veg."

Marj studied her with narrowed eyes. "I'm trying to picture it."

Laureen avoided her gaze. "I did some reading. Swam and lay about."

"Um-hum. Read the latest bestsellers, did you?"

"Umm." Bestsellers had no appeal. She'd spent the time reading psychology texts and studying a couple of child-care models. Something she wasn't about to admit to her co-worker just yet.

"You might fool some of the people all of the time and all of the people some of the time, but you don't fool me." The older woman slid another tray of cookies into the oven and poured herself a mug of coffee before sitting across from Laureen. "So what do you have there?" She nodded at the thick file Laureen had dropped on the table.

"Let's call the boys for milk and cookies; then I'll show you." If she admitted she'd spent hours evaluating case plans for each of the boys, Marj would crow with triumph. Laureen was anxious to present her ideas, but she welcomed a delay, hoping it would give Marj a chance to forget this conversation.

At Laureen's call the boys raced in, all arms and legs, Michael and Davey chattering like a pair of magpies, Kyler smiling and nodding.

Laureen hugged each boy as he passed, breathing in the scent of hot, dusty bodies. She held each of them a bit longer than usual until they wriggled away. This was where she belonged—loving these kids, helping them conquer their pasts, preparing them to meet their futures. She blinked back a tear and sniffed as she straightened.

Marj smiled. "It's good to have you back."

Laureen nodded. "It's good to be back." There was no place like home—especially this home. And there wasn't a better place to plant such a home than right here in Freetown, Alberta. Small-town feel, supportive community, pleasant surroundings. A place where kids could feel safe and learn to trust again.

Not quite as supportive as it had been, she amended, remembering the man next door. She wondered if having Pete as a neighbor was going to make small-town Alberta just a little less trouble free than it had been. Determinedly she pushed the idea away and went to the fridge. She was worrying over nothing. After all, how hard would it be to keep the boys away from him?

Plenty hard, she knew, if they got it in their cute little heads to see what was so all-fired important over there that Pete warned them away. On the other hand there was no point in borrowing trouble. As if she needed to. There was always lots of it around this place.

She poured each boy a glass of milk and passed the cookies. She gave Michael and Davey a big hug when they said "please" and "thank you" without being prompted. And when Kyler made a noise indicating his pleasure and gratitude, she cheered. It might be a long way from a normal six-year-old response, but, compared to the stoically silent boy who had first entered the home, these fledgling attempts at verbal communication were a tremendous improvement.

At the sound of footsteps at the back entry, Marj parted the café curtains and looked out. "Well, would you look at that? Our new neighbor is coming over. He must have smelled the cookies." She hustled to the cupboard for another mug, but Laureen shivered.

The boys seemed blithely interested in nothing more than the snack, but Laureen wasn't convinced. Somehow she didn't think Pete Long was here for milk and cookies.

Wondering what she was in for, she hurried to the back door. Through the screen the man looked stern and forbidding. The creases in his cheeks deepened toward the tightness at the corner of his mouth.

"I knew it," she muttered. "I just knew it." Was there any chance some of Marj's fresh cookies would soften him up? She doubted it would be that easy.

Pushing aside a feeling of doom, she concentrated on smiling welcomingly as she pulled the door open. "Come on in. We were just having coffee."

"I think we need to talk. It won't take more than a minute of your time."

She tried not to grimace, but the man certainly had the ability to look stern.

Searching for her friendliest smile, she stepped aside. "Come on in." She waved him toward a chair.

He stepped into the room, his gaze checking out each boy.

Davey scoped out the man for a second, then returned to his cookies. To an outsider things might have seemed innocent, but Laureen saw the three pairs of feet under the chairs stop swinging and noted how Kyler nibbled at his cookie.

She knew she was in trouble. The question was, how bad?

The quiet shivered up and down Laureen's spine; then Marj

set a cup of coffee at the empty spot on the table. "You're just in time for cookies right out of the oven."

"Thanks." Pete sat but continued looking from one boy to the next.

Three pairs of feet swung in bike-peddling haste.

Laureen was about to say something scintillating—just as soon as she thought of it—when Pete cleared his throat. Three little boys gulped. Davey and Kyler bent lower over their now-empty glasses while Michael scowled at Pete.

"I think you boys have something you need to tell Laureen." He took a cookie and bit into it. "Good cookies," he said, deep dimples flashing in his cheeks as he smiled at Marj.

She grinned. "World's best."

He turned back to the boys. Laureen could almost feel sorry for them the way he studied them so unblinkingly. Not that the two younger ones noticed. They avoided looking anywhere except at the top of the table directly below their noses. As for Michael, after one glance, he settled back into his chair, fists clenched in his lap.

Sensing things were about to erupt, Laureen decided enough was enough. "Michael, have you boys been up to mischief?"

Michael frowned at her. "I don't know what he's talking about."

Pete opened his mouth to speak, but Laureen held up her hand to stall him.

"I'd sooner hear it from you than from Mr. Long," she said to the boys. "Davey, Kyler?"

The younger boys lifted their heads, eyes wide.

Seeing the silent confession on their faces, Michael took control. "We went into his yard again."

Laureen nodded. "I see. Just into his yard? You didn't do anything but go in? Nothing more?"

Three little heads ducked.

Laureen sighed. She'd do anything to avoid trouble with the neighbors, especially a certain one who left her feeling tongue-tied and gauche. She took a deep breath to calm herself.

So what if he gave the impression of unmovable strength? Something she suddenly and unexpectedly craved.

What was the matter with her? He was only a man. She'd seen plenty of them in all shapes and sizes, most recently at the lake.

No doubt that was part of her problem. Every man she'd seen on her holiday was part of a couple—walking hand in hand or sitting at a small table, head bent toward the woman across from him. Watching the couples made her realize how alone she was. Almost isolated. She'd put it down to missing her work.

Now that she was back at work, she could forget those feelings.

Her next-door neighbor sat across the table, hands cradling his cup, to all appearances patiently waiting for someone to say something.

That someone would be me, she decided. "What did they do?"

"Upset my lumber pile." He drank his coffee with all the soberness of a judge imparting a sentence.

Her breath whooshed out. She'd had visions of major vandalism. Graffiti on the garage wall. Or a fire in the middle of the lawn. "That's it?"

He set his cup down with a firmness that made her squirm as much as any of the boys. She had no intention of giving him a chance to explain about trespassing or damages and jumped in with both feet before he could speak.

"I don't mean you shouldn't mind. They shouldn't have been over there, and they know it. Don't you, boys?" Three heads nodded vigorously. Three pairs of eyes pleaded silently for her to be lenient. "In fact, I think we'll have to discuss some form of—" She broke off, deliberately leaving the sentence unfinished. It wouldn't hurt them to wonder what was going to happen. Maybe a little mental suffering would nip this business in the bud.

"Marj, would you take the boys out to play while Mr. Long and I discuss this?" At the tense look in Kyler's eyes she squeezed his shoulder and whispered in his ear, "We're not going to hurt you, honey." Knowing the other two had heard, she smiled reassuringly and patted their backs as they followed Marj out the door.

two

Pete waited as Laureen spoke to the boys. All he wanted was to make it understood his place was off-limits. How hard could it be to watch three little boys? It was her job.

When he'd bought the house, he'd been told of the group home next door. At first he'd balked. Then the couple who owned the house had said not to worry; it was only little boys, and they'd had no trouble with them. None at all. *Hmm. Wonder how much truth was in their words.* So far he'd had plenty of trouble. Seems every time he turned around they were sneaking in or out. And now this. He didn't want to make matters worse. But neither did he want to have to wonder about his stuff or worry that one of them might be injured. This was Freetown. People didn't bother to put everything under lock and key. And he didn't want to have to start doing so, but the way things were going. . .

Laureen hugged the smaller boy. The one with the lighter coloring. The kid seemed to have lost his voice as a result of guilt over his part in the mess in Pete's yard. Or perhaps it was because of her attention.

He studied her over the rim of his cup. Dark hair bouncing away from her shoulders in a flip and catching the light in glittering strands. And there was something unusual about her eyes. Blue and shining, like liquid love pouring out unfettered. When had he ever seen a more beautiful smile?

He took a gulp of coffee that went down too hard.

Marj headed outside, and Laureen talked to the boys. She touched the two older ones on the back, her palms almost holding them. As if she couldn't get enough of them.

His interest grew. These kids weren't even hers.

"Now." She nodded as she returned to the chair across from him. "Let's talk."

Slowly he set his cup down. "It seems to me the boys should be taught to stay in their own yard." He hadn't meant to say it like that. He knew they must be a handful. These kinds of kids always were.

"They are taught." Her smile seemed to carry no animosity. In fact she seemed amused. Not a bit unhappy or sorry about her failure. "But teaching and enforcing are two entirely different things."

"Well, they can't keep getting into my things."

"I agree. I hope they haven't done any damage."

"Nothing serious." No senseless destruction. It looked more like a good dose of curiosity. They just had to find out what he kept under the tarp. It must have been a real disappointment to find nothing but wood. Laureen insisted he tell her precisely what they'd done. "It's not a big deal," he concluded. "As long as they stay out of my yard from now on."

"I'll certainly do my best. But I think they must be held accountable for trespassing and upsetting the lumber pile."

"For sure."

She nodded. "The least they can do is stack it all back. I will personally supervise and make sure they do it right. Is that okay?"

"Okay with me." He'd no sooner said the words than he wondered what had come over him. He'd come to make it clear his yard was off-limits. Now he was practically inviting them back. How had that happened?

He put the last mouthful of cookie in his mouth. They really were great. He'd blame his loss of rational behavior on the delicacies. Fresh from the oven. Almost too good to be real.

And the drawings tacked to the bulletin board. It was all so—so—well, it was like a home. And what did he expect? A hospital? He didn't know. All he knew was this was not a family. These kids were not ordinary kids. They had destructive possibilities beyond the imagination of most kids.

So why was he letting them back into his yard? He needed his head examined.

*

"Hurry up." Michael waved to the other boys to follow as he raced down the alley toward Pete's house.

Laureen narrowed her eyes as she followed them. They seemed awfully eager to be off to do a chore.

They exploded through the gate and skidded to a halt.

Laureen followed, feeling only slightly less disheveled than the three panting boys.

Pete waited, standing there as if he were bracing himself for a storm.

Laureen grinned. The three boys did sort of take one by storm. She clapped her hands. "Okay, boys. You're going to clean up this mess." It wasn't as bad as she imagined. Varying lengths of lumber tumbled across the ground behind the garage. A blue tarpaulin lay folded neatly against the wall. The scent of pine and cedar filled the air.

Pete held out three pairs of gloves. "Put these on first. No point in getting a sliver."

The boys took the leather gloves. Three pairs of hands disappeared into gloves way too big for them.

Michael, eager to be the first ready, reached for a board, and the gloves fell from his hands.

The other two, faces set in serious expression, held their hands aloft to keep the gloves on.

Laureen chuckled. They looked like surgeons about to remove some vital organ.

Pete met her eyes and grinned so briefly she wondered if she had dreamed it; then he bent and grabbed the end of a board, his arms cording with muscles. "Michael, help me put this on the pile."

Laureen practically stared. When was the last time she'd seen Michael move with such eagerness? He grabbed the end of the board and carried it to what remained of the stack.

The two younger boys, not to be left out, grabbed a smaller board and followed. Davey tripped. It was like watching a house of cards tumble down. Davey dropped the board as he went to his knees. Kyler's eyes grew wide as the board jerked out of his grasp. He stumbled and fell backward. The board flipped upright then crashed down on the ground with a thunk. Kyler sat on his seat looking as if he might cry. Davey's eyes glazed over. Michael glowered at Pete.

Pete curled his fists and planted them on his hips. His expression remained impassive. "Okay, fellas. We better get organized. "You"—he pointed to Michael—"move those to one side. You"—he nodded to Davey—"you stack up those shorter pieces. And you"—he curled a finger at Kyler—"you can help me pick up these longer pieces."

They scampered to do his bidding.

Laureen watched them work.

The boys concentrated on following his instructions. Every board had to be just right. And each time they straightened, they glanced to Pete to see his reaction. Apart from the occasional "Good job," he simply nodded. But it seemed as if the boys thought it was a touch from heaven. She'd never seen them work so cheerfully. Or seem so eager to please.

Laureen studied Pete more closely. Something about this man appealed to them. He didn't fawn over them trying to make them like him. In fact he hardly smiled, but his sternness wasn't unfriendly. It seemed, instead, to radiate patience and understanding.

They were almost finished. Michael pushed at the end of a board to align it precisely in the stack. Davey nudged the pile with the toe of his shoe as if to say, "There. Stay in place."

Pete stepped back, Kyler at his side.

Laureen smiled as she saw Kyler's stance and his hands in the too-big-gloves planted on his hips—a perfect imitation of the way Pete stood.

"Let's cover it up, and then we're done," Pete said.

As they moved away, Kyler picked up something. From where she stood, Laureen thought it looked like knots out of the wood.

Kyler turned them over and over. He gave Pete a furtive glance then sighed and dropped them.

"You can have them," Pete said. "Anything on the ground you boys can take. It's just scrap."

Kyler retrieved the two knots, walked slowly across the yard, his gaze on the ground until he found what he wanted and picked up another small piece.

Michael—and Davey, under Michael's direction—found long thin pieces and challenged each other to a sword fight.

"Let's finish first," Pete said.

By the time they had unfolded the tarp and covered the pile

securely, a plan was born in Laureen's mind.

Over the fence she saw Marj come out and called her over. "Boys, you go home with Marj, and she'll get you a drink."

"Thanks for your help," Pete said. He turned to Laureen. "Would you care for something? Coffee? A soft drink?"

"Something cold would be nice, thanks." *Perfect,* she thought. *This will give me a chance to talk to him and get his help.*

ॐ

Pete grabbed two cans of soda from the fridge and hurried back to the patio where Laureen sat waiting. Now that the little guys were gone, he could concentrate on her. Instead of concentrating on not thinking about her. Which was pretty hard to do. She seemed to be everywhere. Helping one of the boys. Giving a word of encouragement. Smiling. Laughing. There was something about the way she poured her love and affection on those kids that made him want to know her better. He handed her the drink and sat across from her, feeling suddenly tongue-tied when she smiled at him, her blue eyes flashing.

"Thanks." She snapped open the can. "You're very good with the kids, you know. I've never seen them so cooperative and eager."

He didn't think he was different from most people. "I treated them as I would any of my men."

Her smile widened. "I guess that's why they respond so well to you. You make them feel grown-up and responsible." She tipped her head and studied him. He liked it that she didn't hide her curiosity by looking at him through her eyelashes. Nor did she look away from his own steady assessment. It was hard to guess her age. Late twenties? Early thirties? She seemed to have a knowledge in her eyes beyond her years. No doubt she'd learned some hard lessons working with these kids.

Then she sat up straighter. "Have you had experience working with kids?"

"Me? Un-uh."

"What do you do with all that wood?" She nodded toward the now-tarped stack. "You a carpenter or something?"

"It's only a hobby."

"What do you make?"

"I'll show you."

She jumped to her feet. "Great."

He opened the garage door and waved an arm. "My shop." What would she think of his fine tools and the projects he had underway?

The first thing she saw was the clock he was making as a gift for his parents.

"You did this?" She bent over it a few minutes then turned and saw the piece he was carving. It was only a simple bird figure. Supposed to be an owl, but carving wasn't as easy as it looked. She picked it up and ran her finger along the shape. "It feels so light." She circled the shop, studying each tool, asking him about them.

Then she was back facing him. "This is only a hobby?"

He nodded. "I'm a plumber by trade."

"Really? Looks to me like you could make a living doing this sort of thing. What took you into plumbing?"

"My parents wanted me to be a dentist like my uncle Manly." He laughed. "I said I'd sooner stick my hands in sewer pipes than in people's mouths." He shrugged. "So I did. For a while anyway. Now I do prefab setups for new construction. It's a good business." He told her about the crew who worked under him and the contracts he had.

Suddenly he realized how much he'd talked about himself. Yet she seemed genuinely interested.

They wandered back to the patio and sat drinking their soda. He leaned back enjoying the peace of his backyard. "What about you? What brought you into your work?"

"I was raised in a fine Christian family. I knew everyone wasn't as fortunate as I was, but the year I was in eighth grade I became good friends with Gina, a foster girl who was my age. My aunt and uncle were her foster parents. Our homes were on the same block so we practically lived in each other's houses."

She looked down at her soda can as she turned it back and forth. "Gina told me what it was like to be moved from place to place. I still hear the pain in her voice when she said she could usually count on being moved just before Christmas or summer holidays."

Pete wanted to reach out and still her trembling fingers as the soda can turned faster and faster. *Yeah,* he derided himself. *That would no doubt settle her tension real quick. A touch from a stranger should be enough to make her bolt out of her chair and run for home.*

" 'It's because no one wants somebody else's kid to ruin their holiday,' Gina said. 'No one wants us forever.' I actually cried when she said she'd give anything to belong somewhere."

Laureen shivered then pushed the pop can aside and leaned back in her chair. She smiled, but her eyes didn't gleam the way they did when she smiled at the kids.

"I said it would be different with my aunt and uncle. They were Christians. I knew they wouldn't send her away for such a silly reason. 'I promise you it won't happen here,' I told her." Her smile dipped at the corners. "I believed in forever after and happy endings. 'Maybe they'll adopt you,' I said." She held his gaze, never looking away though he could sense how emotional her memories were.

"Then they were offered a baby. I guess there were rules that said you couldn't have a foster child and adopt a baby at the same time." Her lips quivered. "I cried and cried when they told me. I begged my aunt to change her mind. But it didn't make a difference."

She pulled her lips into a frown and lifted her eyebrows as she shrugged. "In the end I couldn't keep my promise, and Gina was sent away." Her expression grew stubborn. "That's when I decided I would work with kids who needed a home. I would be different. I wouldn't put my desires above the needs of any child. I would do everything I could to see they got some sort of permanency." She nodded once, emphatically. "I work very hard at finding adoptive homes for these kids and preparing them for that."

Pete dropped his chair to all fours with a thunk. "You really think these kids will ever fit into a normal home? Have you any idea how disruptive they can be to a family?" Even though he kept his gaze fixed firmly on the garage wall, he could feel her start of surprise.

"I can't promise a perfect ending, but I sincerely believe a Christian home with a blend of flexibility and structure can offer love and healing to these kids. That is my hope and prayer."

Pete nodded slowly. He didn't want to appear cold and unsympathetic, but as far as he could tell reality was a long way from the ideal she held. "It'll only work if the child wants to make it work."

"Only partly true. Part of my job, part of the job of both foster and adoptive parents, is to prove to these children it's worthwhile for them to make the effort to work things out because we're there for the long run. We aren't going to pull the rug out from under them the minute things start looking bad. Or good. Unless they can be certain of that why would they even try?"

"Sometimes it isn't enough." He heard the harsh note in his voice and hoped she hadn't noticed. He could feel her studying him but couldn't bring himself to face her.

"What do you know about it?" Her words should have rung with censure or defiance. Instead they were a soft invitation to share. Slowly he turned to meet her gaze.

"My uncle adopted a child like one of those." He jerked his head toward the home. "And believe me—it was not a happily-ever-after story."

three

Laureen sat quietly as he told his story. His uncle had adopted an eight-year-old boy when his own two children were eleven and twelve. The child manipulated the uncle and took advantage of his good nature until finally the older children rebelled and left home.

"It cost my uncle his family and his marriage. And for what? As far as I know Billy is in jail. It ruined the family. My uncle is now a lonely old man in a nursing home. He has early Alzheimer's, and none of his family will visit him. For a while it even shook my faith in God. Why would He allow such a thing to happen?"

"But you're okay now?"

"Of course."

The silence settled around them. Laureen sighed. "There are no guarantees, but most of these children can be salvaged if people are willing to give them a fair chance."

He gave her a steady look. "I hope you're right." He shook his head slowly. "But I don't think I'd be willing to take the risk. After all, it's not as if the child belongs to me."

"I guess lots of people feel the same way which is why we try as much as possible to find relatives willing to take these kids." She thought about his experience with adoption. Maybe if he would listen to her idea and agree to it, he would overcome the bad memories he had and look at these kids in a different light.

"You have a lot to offer the boys. You have skill with your hands. You have patience in working with them. They'd really benefit from having a man spend some time with them." She paused and gathered her breath for her sell job. "I was wondering if you'd consider taking on a project with them. Maybe teach them some simple woodworking skills. Or—" At the look on his face, she broke off.

"You must be kidding. I have no desire to be part of your absolution. Besides, I'm too busy."

She jerked to her feet. "Absolution? Is that what you think this is? Is that how you see my work? Selfish vainglory? You think I'm suffering from a guilt complex? Well, you couldn't be more wrong." She pulled herself tall and straight. "And we'll get along fine without any help from you." Her back rigid, she marched out of his yard, her eyes fixed straight ahead until she reached her own back door where she took a deep breath, and with the strength of purpose she had developed over her years of working in the home, she pulled herself together before she faced the kids.

Why had she let him upset her? It didn't matter an ounce what he thought. He wasn't the first person to assign weird motives to her for her work. Who cared if for a moment or two she'd wondered if they could work together on something and maybe get to know each other better? After that little episode she hoped she'd never lay eyes on him again.

❧

It had been easy to almost shut Pete from her mind. Life had a way of consuming all her time, leaving her little opportunity to think about the man next door.

Michael and Davey had gone to camp for two weeks, and Marj had gone on holiday, leaving her alone with Kyler. She'd purposely planned it that way in hopes some intense one-on-one would help him open up.

But neither work nor relaxation made it possible to forget Pete completely. She heard his door slam as he left in the morning. She heard his phone ring when he had the cordless outside. She heard the hum and screech of his power tools and felt a pang that he wouldn't give some of his time to the boys. She prayed for his emotional healing even as she prayed the boys would find healing, love, and permanent homes. She nodded to him when she saw him in church or on the sidewalk, but their interests were too far apart for anything more.

She spent several minutes praying for God's guidance with her work before she called Kyler into the little bedroom she'd converted into a lounge for the next few weeks. Her plan meant talking to him nearly every waking moment of the day hoping she would find some topic to trigger a response from him.

Or, she grinned to herself, maybe he'd start talking in self-defense just to shut her up.

From a box of small toys Kyler chose some trucks and cars to play with as she talked. He pulled the three little pieces of wood he'd picked up in Pete's yard from his pocket and set them in the middle of the table then proceeded to circle the vehicles around them.

She racked her brain for more stories to share with Kyler. Over the past few days she'd told him about her brothers and things the three of them had done together.

She'd told about how one brother took apart the engine in her dad's old truck one day without her dad's permission. And hid the fact for weeks as he tried to put it back together.

She'd talked about the pets they'd had, the outings they took, the camping trips, and the visits to a friend's farm.

She knew he listened for he smiled at appropriate times. And she was certain he enjoyed the stories because he often made happy Winnie-the-Pooh-Bear sounds.

But he never spoke a word.

Lord, she prayed as she searched her mind for more stories, *heal this little boy. Please let him say something. Just one word.*

She thought of a dream she used to have.

"I would be on something tall, like the cupboard, or looking out a window or standing on the bank of a ravine," she told him. "And then I would fall. I don't think I ever hit the ground, but I remember being so scared and trying to grab something—the wall or a bush—anything to keep from falling. Then I would wake up sweating and so scared I'd be afraid to go back to sleep." She hadn't thought of it in years. Like so many things, especially childhood fears, it had faded and disappeared from her mind.

"You still afraid?" a tiny voice whispered.

Laureen had been sprawled out, her legs stretched under the table; but when she heard the whisper she sat up so fast she cracked her knee against the table leg and grabbed at it. But the pain registered only peripherally as she stared at Kyler, half thinking she'd imagined his question. She wanted to cheer but was afraid any burst of excitement would put an end to his saying more so she only looked at him keenly.

His expression anxious, he waited for her answer.

"No, I'm not afraid of falling anymore. You know why?" *Please, God—I said one word, but now I want just one more. I want to be sure I heard him.*

"Why?" he whispered.

Thank You, God. Oh, thank You. She thought she might explode any minute.

"My mother had me memorize a Bible verse. It was from Psalm 56, verse 3. 'When I am afraid, I will trust in you.' That means I will trust God to look after me." He nodded. "I said it over and over, and after awhile the dreams stopped."

He looked at her solemnly then glanced at the door. He'd had enough. Or maybe he wanted to be alone to think about everything. No doubt speaking out loud for the first time in two years had taken a lot of nerve. And energy.

"Do you want to go out and play now?"

He scooped up the pieces of wood and ran outside. She watched until he settled down in the sandpile, then let out a subdued cheer.

If only Marj were home so she could share the news with someone. She heard the sound of a motor next door and knew Pete had returned from work.

She had to share her news or burst, and she hurried to the fence hoping to catch him before he went inside. He stood with his key in hand as she peered over the fence.

"How about a cup of coffee?" she called. When he hesitated, she added, "I'm feeling in need of some adult company." Sure, make it sound like she was desperate.

He waited for the space of a heartbeat, then nodded. "I could use some java about now." He pocketed his keys and strode toward the back gate.

"Bad day at work?" she asked.

"Sort of. The supplies I needed to meet a contract deadline didn't come in, so I've had to scramble to find another supplier. And now we'll all have to put in overtime to complete the work." He shrugged and gave a weary smile. "It's just one of those things."

"I'm sorry. Maybe coffee will help." She poured them each

a cupful, and they sat at the kitchen table where she could watch Kyler play. "Maybe my good news will cheer you up."

He looked at her expectantly. "Good news? I could certainly stand to hear some."

"Then you're in luck." She leaned forward, not one bit shy about her wide grin. "Today Kyler said"—she held up her hand with the fingers splayed out—"four words."

He looked puzzled. "He doesn't talk?"

"Not for two years." She told him the circumstances. "But we knew he could. We've heard him whispering on the monitor after he's in bed. But apart from the sounds he makes to indicate certain things, this is the first time he's spoken to any of us." She wrapped her arms around her shoulders and hugged herself. "I am so happy. I have prayed for a breakthrough this week." She sighed loudly. "If this is the beginning of his really talking we can look at his placement." It was with mixed feelings she told him about the young couple planning to adopt him. She was glad he would be going to a permanent family, but this child, more than any other she'd worked with, had taken over a part of her heart. "It will be hard to see him go," she admitted.

"Where are the others?" Pete asked, and she explained.

"Why don't you join us for supper since we're both alone?" she said.

He sighed. "Sounds great. I was wondering how I'd face making myself something nutritious. I decided I just didn't feel up to it and hoped there'd be a nuke-and-scarf supper in the freezer."

She chuckled at his description of a frozen meal.

"I accept." He lifted his hand. "One condition, though. You let me help."

"You're on." Suddenly the prospect of supper seemed a lot more appealing.

Pete washed the new potatoes she'd purchased earlier in the day while she cut the steak into pieces for shish kebabs. While the potatoes cooked, they worked together preparing peppers, zucchini, mushrooms, and cherry tomatoes and threading them on the skewers.

As they washed and diced vegetables, Pete explained more about his job. After awhile his talk turned to family. "My parents have left their professional lives and live on a back-to-nature acreage north of Vancouver." She laughed as he told stories of his parents trying to cope with no water, no sewer, and no electricity. "They'd starve if they truly lived like that, but when their efforts fail, they run out to the grocery store and buy what they need. Of course"—he gave her one of those slow smiles of his, his eyes dipping at the corners—"they ride their bikes so in their minds it still qualifies as living off the land."

Laureen laughed. She'd have never guessed he could be so amusing. He had the sort of face that didn't give away his emotions unless one looked closely. That's when she noticed the deepening of the creases in his cheeks, the twinkling in his eyes. In fact, when she studied him, she decided he had one of the kindest faces she'd ever seen. Suddenly aware of how closely she'd been scrutinizing him, she ducked her head. "Do you have siblings?" She concentrated on seasoning the shish kebabs, but at his sardonic chuckle she looked at him again.

"Maybe they're the reason my parents have escaped to the stump farm." Seeing her puzzled expression, he continued. "My brother is still trying to find himself. Which means he ventures into wild schemes, and when they fail he borrows money, desperate to get himself out." He snorted. "I use the term 'borrow' very loosely."

Laureen grinned. "I've had a few friends like that."

"And my sister. What can I say that doesn't sound like I'm bad-mouthing her?" He thought for a moment. "She's into serial disastrous love affairs. Every time one fails, she wails and cries and says she's going to become a nun, but within a month or two, she's found the next perfect solution to her problems. In a long line of supposedly perfect solutions." He shook his head. "No wonder Mom and Dad moved away. I'm the most normal one of the bunch."

"Do your brother and sister make you feel like moving, too?"

"Nope. I soon learned to say no to them. After awhile they stopped asking. Now they drop by for an occasional visit. I'm glad to see them come and even more glad to see them go."

They carried the skewered food to the barbecue and stood side by side, talking as they tended the food on the grill.

"My parents still live in the same house I grew up in," she said. "And it seems my brothers started on their chosen courses early in life." She'd told Kyler about her brothers, and now she told Pete. "Stuart went from taking my dad's vehicles apart to become a mechanic. Drew went from fiddling around with our computer to become a computer engineer."

"And you went from wanting to keep Gina safe and close to helping other kids feel safe."

She wondered if he was mocking her, but his smile was so gentle she felt like hugging herself.

"I do what I can."

"I'd guess you do pretty well at it; otherwise Kyler wouldn't have felt safe enough with you to talk."

She wanted to hug him for affirming her. She knew Kyler's progress was the result of a group effort—the combined efforts of all the staff and the psychologist. And it was an answer to much prayer. But she liked to think she'd had special input in the journey. She'd spent the last two years pouring love and affection on this child. And for him to say his first words to her. . .

She laughed with joy.

"I'm so glad I could help him."

The food was cooked and the picnic table set. She called Kyler. He ambled over, nodding hello to Pete.

"Would you say the blessing?" she asked Pete. When he readily agreed, then prayed a simple prayer of gratitude that included Kyler, Laureen's attitude toward him took an abrupt upturn. He was really a very nice man.

Before Kyler touched his food, he arranged his three pieces of wood before his plate.

"He has sure enjoyed playing with that wood you gave him," Laureen said as she passed the butter for Pete to slather over his potatoes.

Pete looked surprised then picked up each piece of wood and studied it. A slow smile deepened the creases in his cheeks as he set the pieces back precisely as Kyler had placed them. "Looks like Poppa, Momma, and Baby Woodknot."

Kyler nodded vigorously making pleased little sounds.

Laureen blinked. "I never noticed." This man had no idea how astute he was with kids. What a shame. She'd give anything to get him to work with the boys. At least Kyler, for she couldn't help but notice Kyler seemed at ease with Pete. If only he would—but he'd already said no. She could pray God would change his mind, though.

ঌ

Pete sat outside on his patio, nursing a can of soda. Peace and quiet. This was the kind of place he thought of when he thought of home and family. And lately he'd been thinking of home and family a lot. Not his parents and siblings, though they were okay in their own way, if somewhat eccentric at times. No, he'd been thinking about a family of his own. He'd concentrated on work until now, coming up through the ranks of plumbing, all the time thinking and planning this business of his. Now that he had it established he could focus in a different direction. Time to settle down and start a family.

Of course he needed to find the right woman first. A pair of sparkling blue eyes, a wide smile, and a generous laugh sprang to mind, and he glanced at the house next door.

Nah. Not Laureen. She was cute and friendly and happy, but not the sort of woman for him. He wanted someone—he paused and scratched his head—what did he want? Someone steady, ready to settle down with him to raise a family. Someone who would love him enthusiastically.

He smiled at his choice of words. Again, a mental picture of Laureen popped into his head. She certainly loved those boys enthusiastically. Seemed she was always hugging one or patting another on the back or shoulders, almost like a benediction. And she rejoiced over every little thing they did. Yes, she was certainly free with her love. But she shared it with all those kids. It might sound selfish, but he didn't want a shared love. Besides he kind of gathered she was married to her job. She hardly ever talked about anything else, and he'd never seen anyone visiting next door who could even remotely be considered a boyfriend. When he saw her in church, she was always alone. If one could call having the boys with her alone.

No, not his type of woman at all. He wanted someone with eyes and heart for no one but him. And whatever children they had together.

Most of all he did not want to repeat his uncle Norman's mistake. A wife and children were God-given privileges and responsibilities. Not to be sacrificed for other causes no matter how noble.

Part of the reason he'd moved to Freetown was to be closer to the nursing home where his uncle Norman was a resident. Pete visited several times a week—the only visitor his uncle ever had. His own family had cut off all ties because of Billy's destructive behavior and his uncle's determination to salvage the boy. He'd chosen Billy over his own family. And for what? Billy never called or sent a card, either.

Uncle Norman became quite agitated when he tried to talk of his family. The only thing that calmed him was for Pete to open the Bible and read.

He studied the fence separating the two yards. It was awfully quiet with Michael and Davey gone. He lifted a corner of his mouth in a self-mocking grin. Guess there was one advantage in having a kid who didn't talk. It was quiet.

Too quiet.

Maybe they weren't even home. He strained to catch any sounds to indicate someone was around next door. He thought he heard music from deep inside the house. And then a soft thud in the yard. It could have been anything.

He wandered across to the fence and looked over.

Kyler stood in the middle of the yard with a striped ball. He sighed as if the whole world had abandoned him, then threw the ball toward the back gate with as much enthusiasm as Pete felt when he had to go to the doctor. He waited for the ball to bounce back; then, sighing again, he shuffled over and retrieved it.

Pete grinned. Kyler didn't need words to communicate how tired he was of playing alone. Pete wondered where Laureen was and half expected to see the door burst open and her run out, bubbling with enthusiasm and offering to play with him.

But the boy threw the ball again and with another loud sigh retrieved it.

Pete couldn't stand it any longer and went out the gate and down the alley.

He stepped into the yard and faced Kyler. "Want to play catch?" He cupped his hands, calmly ignoring the inconsistency of his actions—saying he didn't want to be involved with these kids and then offering to play ball with one of them.

Kyler grinned wide enough to swallow his head and threw the ball. It was a little off center, and Pete had to dive for it, landing on his arm.

"Ohh," he grunted as he bolted to his feet. "You trying to kill me?"

Kyler giggled. And Pete stood grinning at him with an enjoyment he hadn't felt in many days.

He lobbed the ball toward the boy in a slow arc. Kyler opened his arms and caught it, his pleased expression making Pete chuckle.

"Good catch."

They tossed the ball back and forth, both laughing when Pete did an exaggerated dive to catch a wild toss or pretended the ball he caught in the stomach took his breath away.

He was poised to catch another toss when he heard the

screen door slap and almost tripped over himself.

"I see you have company," Laureen said to Kyler. When Pete brought his gaze to meet hers, she added, "Thank you." Her bright smile choked his thoughts like a vise.

He wiped the back of his arm across his forehead.

"Sorry, Kyler. I didn't mean to be so long." She faced Pete again. "I promised him I'd play ball with him, but I had to get the bills organized. But now you're here we can play three-cornered catch." She clapped her hands, then held them out inviting Pete to toss the ball.

He did. Slow and gentle as he would for Kyler.

She threw the ball to the boy.

He saw the mischief in Kyler's face before the boy threw one as hard as any before. Pete knew what was expected of him and caught the ball, letting his arms carry the movement into his stomach; then he bent over and moaned.

"You trying to cripple me so I can't go to work?"

Kyler giggled.

Understanding that he was teasing, Laureen laughed. "Better be careful, Kyler. You hurt him, and you'll have to go do his work for him."

The boy giggled some more and bounced up and down.

Pete balanced the ball on the palm of his hand as he studied Laureen.

She grinned wickedly and planted her feet apart. She bent over at her waist and wobbled back and forth. "Come on, Pete. Give me a good one." She smacked her fist into her palm. "Right here. Give 'er all you got."

He rolled the ball up and down his wrist then slowly wound up and let the ball sail in an easy toss.

She caught it in one hand and snorted. "That the best you

can do?" She gave him a disdainful look as she threw the ball toward Kyler. "Sissy stuff."

Kyler caught the ball and, still giggling, aimed it toward Pete.

He reached out to catch the toss, but distracted by Laureen's expression, he stumbled and barely managed to keep from falling on his face.

Kyler clapped his hands and bounced.

Pete straightened. Good thing the kid thought it was part of the game. He watched Laureen resume her taunting stance.

"Come on, big boy. Put it right here."

He pressed the ball between his palms. She made it mighty difficult not to take this game seriously.

He squinted and winged the ball toward her, aiming it to the right so she had to reach and jump for it.

"Smarty pants," she murmured. "But you'll have to do better than that. Remember I grew up with two brothers."

He aimed balls to her left and to her right. He sent her low ones and high ones. He had her diving to catch them, but unless he threw them right out of sight she never missed.

Finally she tucked the ball under her arm and flung herself on the ground. "Enough," she said panting. "I'm getting way too hot."

Kyler sprawled on the ground beside her.

Pete remained standing, uncertain what to do. Should he say good-bye and go home? He sure didn't want to. He was having way too much fun. Besides they looked so comfortable and relaxed. Not giving himself a chance to examine his decision, he dropped down on the ground beside Laureen and sat with his knees pulled up, resting the sides of his arms on his knees.

"Man, I worked up a real sweat," she said, shaking the bottom of her shirt. "And a gigantic thirst, but I'm too lazy to go get a drink."

Kyler jumped up and ran to the house, returning in a few minutes with three cans of iced tea.

"Why, thank you, Kyler. How nice of you." She ruffled his hair. He looked as if he would split in two he grinned so wide.

"Yeah. Thanks a lot, kid. You're a good ballplayer."

Kyler's eyes widened, and he made a happy little sound.

Laureen sat up. "Kyler, maybe you want to say thank you to Pete for playing ball with you."

The boy sobered. He looked from Laureen to Pete.

Laureen laid her hand over Pete's wrist exerting enough pressure to warn him to wait.

Kyler nodded and licked his lips once. "Thank you," he whispered.

A lump settled in the back of Pete's throat. He didn't know how much of this he could take. Kyler choosing to speak to him. Laureen's hand touching his. He wasn't one to get all emotional, but a man could stand just so much.

He cleared his throat and found his voice. "My pleasure, Kyler." He chucked the kid on the arm and was rewarded with a huge grin.

"It looks like a good evening for a wiener roast," Laureen said, pulling her hand away. "Pete, would you like to join us?"

Kyler grabbed Pete's hand and nodded vigorously.

"Would you like me to stay, Kyler?"

The boy's eyes shone as he nodded again.

Pete looked at him, waiting.

Kyler saw what he wanted. "Yes, please," he said, his voice firmer and fuller than before.

An unaccountable pleasure filled Pete. "Then I will." How could he turn down such an invitation? A little boy eager enough to talk to him and a woman with keen blue eyes and a killer smile? It was more than he could resist.

Kyler clapped and plunked down beside Pete.

Laureen looked at the pair of them. "I suppose it would be too much to expect the two of you to help." She sounded exasperated, but the smile in her eyes made it plain she was pleased at how things had gone.

Pete looked at Kyler.

Kyler looked at Pete and waited to see what he would say.

"What do you think, kid? Should we give her a hand?"

His eyes wide, Kyler nodded.

"Okay. We will." Pete jumped to his feet and pulled Kyler to his. "Okay, fine lady, what do you want us to do?"

"There's a portable fire pit in the shed." She nodded toward the barn-shaped structure in the far corner of the yard. "You could bring it out and put it over there." She pointed to a spot close to the picnic table. "And there's firewood there, too. Kyler, will you show Pete?"

Pete paused and grinned at the little boy. "Is she always this bossy?" The way he felt right now she could have ordered him to march around the world and he would immediately start a "hup, two, three, four" without even pausing to put on marching boots.

Laureen waved him away. "Of course I am. It's my job."

Pete swung toward the little building with an exaggerated swagger. "Come on, young fella. Show me where everything is."

❧

Pete looked up from where he was using the router to cut a piece of wood to fit around the face of the clock. He was certain he'd seen a shadow slip across the wall, and he jerked around.

Nothing. It must be the tree in the lane swaying in the summer breeze.

Funny he hadn't noticed a shadow from that tree before.

And strange things were happening to his tools as well.

He studied the table where he did his carving. It had happened a number of times. He went out for something, and when he came back a tool was out of place—and he couldn't remember moving it. Of course, it could be he wasn't remembering clearly. Not only his tools seemed to wander. His thoughts wandered a lot, too. He'd be working away when suddenly he'd realize he was smiling for no reason. No reason, that is, except recalling something Laureen had said or done.

He couldn't remember when he'd had more fun than at the wiener roast. They had teased and laughed and told jokes and laughed some more. He'd laughed so much his stomach hurt.

Since then he'd found excuses to go over several more times. Playing catch with Kyler was always a good reason or casually inviting himself over when Laureen came out and sat alone after the boy had gone to bed.

Now where had he put the sandpaper he'd bought this afternoon? Oh, yeah. He'd left it in the house.

A shadow flitted across the door as he returned. He looked around. Not even the tree could have thrown a shadow that far. He shook his head. *Concentrate, man. You're letting your thoughts run away on you.*

He sanded the face of the clock gently, then stained it. While it dried, he returned to carving his owl. He'd be the first to admit he wasn't very good at carving, but he found it relaxing.

He reached for a chisel and stopped, his hand arrested in

midmotion above the table. This time he knew it was not his imagination. The evidence was right there before him.

He picked up the piece of wood and examined it. A squarish shape but one someone had begun to form into a crude figure of a man. He turned it over, admiring how whoever did this had followed the natural grain of the wood so it became part of the figure.

But who could have done it? He kept the shop locked when he was away. Though that wouldn't keep a determined thief out. But his door hadn't been jimmied. Nor was there any damage done.

Whoever had done this was interested in craft, not vandalism or hocking the tools.

Had Laureen seen anything?

Only one way to find out. He palmed the rough figure and locked the door firmly behind him. He checked the lock twice and glanced up and down the lane as he headed next door.

four

Kyler played contentedly with his bucket of cars and trucks as Laureen folded his freshly laundered shirts and pants and daydreamed. This had been an exciting summer.

First they'd acquired a new neighbor, and, second, Kyler had started to talk. Her acquaintance with Pete was taking a turn she was sure neither of them expected. They were slowly becoming friends. Laureen pressed a small red T-shirt to her nose and smiled. Pete might have refused to help with the boys, but he was having an impact on one of them all the same.

God was answering her prayer on Kyler's behalf. Although she couldn't see it yet, she knew He was also working in Pete's life.

Several times she and Pete had talked of spiritual things. He told her more about his uncle. She was surprised to learn he was in a nearby nursing home and even more surprised to discover it was what brought Pete to Freetown.

Pete's voice had grown hoarse when he asked Laureen to pray for his uncle. "He is agitated much of the time. I wish he could be at peace."

She closed her eyes and, with a heart bursting with gratitude, thanked God for all the good things and prayed a special blessing on Pete's uncle.

She glanced up. Through the window she saw Pete crossing the backyard, and her heart leaped. Not waiting for him to knock, she hurried to open the door.

"Welcome, neighbor. Come on in."

He hesitated as if his thoughts had been on something else, then stepped inside. "I came over to see if you'd noticed anyone hanging around my shop."

"No. Can't say I have. Why?" *Please, God, not more mischief.* But with Michael and Davey gone, Kyler seemed content to stay close to home.

"At first I thought I had imagined it, but someone has been in my shop." He shoved a piece of wood at her. "See what I found."

She took the object. Someone had begun to carve it. "This isn't yours?"

He shook his head.

Kyler slipped from the chair and pressed himself into the narrow space between the fridge and the wall. The look on his face said more than a thousand words. Guilt. Plain and simple. But why? When?

She caught Pete's eyes and nodded toward the boy. "I think we've found the culprit. I'm sorry. I had no idea."

She turned toward Kyler. "You know the rule. No going into Pete's yard without permission—and especially no using his tools without his being there. You could get hurt. Please apologize."

Kyler managed a whispered "Sorry" then shrank back into the corner.

But Pete grabbed the piece of wood. "No. No. Look at this. It's amazing a little kid has that sort of talent. See how he uses the natural shape of the wood."

She examined it carefully. Blunt cuts chopped the edges. It had a sort of Gumby shape to it. But Pete was right. For a boy not quite six it was very good. "This is almost good enough to enter in the fall fair." She turned toward Kyler who shrank farther back into the corner. "What do you think? Would you like to do that?"

He nodded once, briskly, his eyes still wide with fright.

"With a little help he could finish it in time." Her voice trailed off. She wanted to ask Pete to help him. But she didn't want to risk their fledgling friendship by requesting something he had already vehemently refused.

God, I sense Your hand in this. I'll be quiet and let You do the work.

Sometimes being quiet was the hardest thing in the world.

"I'm not very good at carving," Pete said, his tone thoughtful. "But I could help him." He seemed to give the crude carving a great deal of study. "This sort of talent should be encouraged." He nodded toward Kyler. "In fact we'll make a whole family. How would you like that, Kyler?"

Laureen blinked as her heart threatened to overflow. *Thank You, God!*

Kyler nodded, his eyes sparkling, and slowly he eased away from the wall. He faced Pete, his small face twisting. Then he touched the carving in Pete's hand and said, "Thank you," before he ducked past the man to run outside.

"He'll go play in the corner of the yard for a while." Laureen explained. "He likes to be alone when he's excited about something. And I can tell you, this is really exciting news for him. Did you see the way his eyes glowed?"

Pete nodded. "The kid has real talent."

"He's a special kid," Laureen agreed, waving Pete inside. "Have a chair while I make coffee." She filled the pot with water and scooped coffee into the basket. "I love all the kids, but Kyler's different. It's the first time I've seriously thought of adopting one of the kids." He'd burrowed right into her heart and grown there. "Always before I've reminded myself I can do more good working for all the kids than devoting myself to one." The coffee sputtered through the filter into the pot. They both watched the level rise. .

"If I adopted a child, could I still pour my energies into helping the steady stream that comes through here or would I want to be home with my own child?"

"I suppose kids spend most of their day at school," Pete said.

"But that's it. I'd want to be home when I needed to be at work. How could I give both the kids in the home and a child of my own adequate attention? But, as I said, with Kyler I almost changed my mind. I guess it's a good thing there are family members ready to adopt him. I've spoken to the couple again and arranged for them to take him on Saturday. It's time to work at getting him settled permanently."

Pete looked thoughtful.

Laureen wondered if he was thinking of his uncle's experience with adopting an older child. She wished she could tell him it would work out. She wished she could know it for sure herself. She couldn't stand to think Kyler would be hurt by the sort of rejection Gina lived with. Even expected.

But when Pete spoke his question had nothing to do with Kyler. "Where do you see yourself in the future?"

The coffee done, she filled two cups, placed them on the table, and sat across from him. She was stalling, but his question had caught her off guard. All her life—at least since eighth grade and her short-lived friendship with Gina—she had promised herself she would put her hand to the task and not turn back.

She lifted her head and smiled at Pete as a sense of purpose and serenity filled her. "Probably still here working with kids and helping them find homes."

His dark eyes narrowed as if displeased with her answer. "Don't you want to get married and have a family of your own?"

She shrugged. "I've committed myself to helping kids." She took a burning gulp of coffee. Never, ever, would she make a selfish choice as her aunt and uncle had done. No way. The kids must always come first.

Pete's gaze settled on some far point. "Somehow I don't see that as being enough. There must be a part of you that longs for a home of your own. Children of your own."

She held her cup firmly, refusing to let his words dig at her. "I suppose it's a basic human desire." She kept her voice light. "What about you? Is that what you want?"

His chest rose and fell sharply. "You bet. I've spent all my life working and building a business. I'm almost thirty. Now I want to settle down. Start a family. Have a real home."

A burning sensation rose in her chest at the way he emphasized "real" home. He was right. This was not a real home. This was a stopgap measure for kids needing real homes. But her work was important.

What would it be like to have my own home? My own kids?

She set her cup down with a thud. She had Pete to thank— to blame—for putting such thoughts in her head. Before he came along she'd never even considered such things. She didn't need unrest in her heart.

Lord, please keep me faithful. Help me focus on the needs of these children.

She slowly filled her lungs, pushing aside selfish thoughts, vowing to concentrate on the task of helping kids. That was her future.

Pete was a nice man—patient and steady and kind. Even more than he knew. She was certain he would make someone a good husband and father. But apart from their fledgling friendship, which she appreciated tremendously, her only interest in him was in getting him to volunteer some time working with the boys.

And God was already answering her prayer in that direction.

But an inner voice rose up in argument. *You won't be content forever helping other people's children.*

She dismissed the idea as quickly as it came.

"So you're happy to work with these kids, then let them go? No regrets?"

His question slammed into her.

She gasped. Did he have any idea how hard it was to let them go? Her fingers curled tightly around her cup. The thought of saying good-bye to Kyler made her eyes sting. "It isn't always easy. But I have to believe it's for the best." Why was he talking like this? His continual prodding was upsetting her equilibrium. Her coffee cup was empty, and she grabbed the pot for refills. Rather than sit down again she looked around the kitchen. "I should think of something for supper."

"Why don't you let me treat for a change?"

∴

Pete could see his questions had upset Laureen. That hadn't been his intention.

So what, he jeered inwardly, *was your intention? Did you hope she'd say she'd drop this job in a moment if the right guy came along?* Did he think he was the right guy?

Okay, so it bothered him that she was willing to pour her life into these transient kids. Kids that would, in all probability, not settle in the permanent homes she worked so hard to get them.

But she chose to believe otherwise. She wouldn't let herself think these kids would not be the answer to prayer for everyone wanting a child.

But it had been clear from the first this was a subject they would never agree on. Their experiences had been too different. She'd seen the needs and disappointments of a child wanting security. He'd seen and experienced secondhand the effects of placing such a child into an unsuspecting family.

He regularly saw the pain his uncle's decision had brought to him and his family. Pete couldn't believe God had wanted his uncle to destroy something so sacred. Second Timothy 5:8, stated, "If anyone does not provide for his relatives, and especially for his immediate family, he has denied the faith and is worse than an unbeliever." It seemed to Pete the message was clear enough. Your own family came first.

Of course, that didn't give him the right to impose his feelings on her. She was doing a good work. And she was good at it. If God chose to use her in that way, she deserved his wholehearted admiration.

Yet he couldn't help thinking—well, it didn't matter what he thought. She'd been honest with him. He appreciated that. And he certainly had no desire to upset her. But he had.

Maybe taking her and Kyler out for supper would bring back the happy gleam to her eyes. Especially if he did his best to be kind and entertaining.

They decided to walk to the nearest hamburger joint for burgers and fries where they sat outside under a big red-and-white umbrella to eat.

He teased Kyler about the way the wind kept tossing his napkin in his fries and was rewarded when the boy chuckled. He was even more rewarded when Laureen ruffled Kyler's hair and gave Pete a grateful smile.

Afterward, walking down the sidewalk on their way back to the home, Pete knew he had succeeded in smoothing things between them. He'd enjoyed their time together and wasn't anxious for the evening to end. He searched for a reason to stretch it out.

"We should plan when Kyler is going to come over and work on his carving."

"Why don't we talk about it as soon as I get him tucked in?" Laureen said.

Could he hope she was as eager as he to prolong their time together? That she wanted to forget about their earlier difference of opinion?

"Sure." He sat on one side of the picnic table. "I'll wait here. Take your time."

Kyler waved good night, and he and Laureen went inside.

Pete leaned on his elbows and prepared to wait. He smiled into the lengthening shadows as he thought of how Laureen had bubbled with enthusiasm as they walked home.

She was full of plans for Kyler's project. Her gratitude for Pete's help made him feel as if he were king of the world.

"I'm back." She brought them each a glass of iced tea and sat down beside him. "Isn't it nice out? The air so soft and cool and smelling of roses and petunias. This is the best part of the day."

He agreed, thinking he'd never enjoyed it so much before.

They talked of many things—the weeks he'd spent at summer camp as a child and how it had shaped his Christian growth, the camping trips the family took to Banff and Jasper.

"I was there the summer that little boy fell into a crevasse and died." It had a tremendous impact on the whole family.

His parents sat in shock all evening. His sister had cried into her pillow half the night. He couldn't remember what his brother did, but he'd stared out the window next to his bunk in the Holiday Trailer. "Over and over I asked God why. He never told me, but somehow it made me learn to trust Him about the future."

"It seems both our lives have been shaped by significant events in our lives—Gina for me, that dreadful accident for you. Though no doubt lots of little things have shaped us, too. Like—" She paused then told him of a recurring dream she used to have of falling. "With God's help I outgrew that."

"I used to dream I was stuck in a culvert." He chuckled. "And then I go into plumbing. Go figure."

"I guess you could have been a dentist." She gave him a teasing look.

He pretended to gag, and she laughed. She had a smile and laugh to die for, and he felt his grin deepen until it slashed right across his heart. He was so glad she'd forgiven him for asking questions that made it sound as if he thought what she was doing was a waste of time.

"How often do you want Kyler to come over for carving lessons?"

Her question brought him back to reality. "Better make it as often as possible if we're to get it done on time." He suggested she bring him over after supper the next day.

five

Next evening Laureen took Kyler next door as soon as the dishes were done.

Pete was in the shop, the carving tools lined up neatly on the table.

Laureen was relieved to see there were no sharp knives. All day she'd worried if she'd done the right thing. Maybe Kyler would cut his finger off. How would she explain that?

Pete greeted her with a warm smile, then turned to Kyler.

She was glad his attention was on the boy. It gave her a chance to watch him unobserved. And he was a pleasure to watch, his expression mobile and fluid as he talked to Kyler. With his patience and slow laugh, Pete was an ideal father figure for all the boys who came through the home. Again she silently thanked God for working it out so he was willing to help Kyler.

"I'll let you pick some wood out of this collection," he said to Kyler. "Then we'll start work."

Kyler lingered over the selection, picking up pieces, examining them then putting them back or setting them aside. Finally he was satisfied.

"Those are what you want?" Pete asked.

Kyler nodded.

Pete curled a finger around the boy's chin and turned the little face toward him. "I'd like to hear you say it."

Kyler looked at Pete with the intensity of a wary wild animal, but Laureen sensed the boy was not afraid, simply measuring the man. "I want these." Then for good measure he added, "Please."

"Good boy." Pete said, his voice deep with emotion.

Tears tickled Laureen's nose at the trusting bond being forged between these two.

"Now"—Pete turned to the tools—"we'll use these chisels and files to shape the wood." Working as he talked, he showed Kyler how to hold the wood all the while explaining safety measures.

Kyler listened intently, his look as eager when he watched Pete working as it was when he was allowed to shape the wood himself.

Laureen stayed in the background fascinated at the way the two of them worked together, almost able to read each other's minds.

Pete let the child tackle the work on his own, and when it seemed too difficult, he quietly guided Kyler's hands.

Laureen pinched the bridge of her nose as tears again threatened. It was such a joy to see them together. Kyler was a special little boy. And Pete was a special man who related instinctively well with the boy. This was so good for Kyler.

And God was answering her prayer in a wonderful way—above and beyond what she could have imagined.

They worked an hour; then Pete called a halt. "Never work so long you start to lose your concentration." He showed Laureen the figure they'd been working on. Already she could see the man taking a more defined shape.

&

Pete thought of Laureen all day, making it impossible to concentrate. Several times he found himself staring at his hands, wondering what he was doing. Finally he threw a wrench on the cement floor of the shop. He marched into his office and slammed the door, ignoring the startled looks of his employees. He fired up his computer, opened his drafting program and fed in some stats for the next job. This sort of work always consumed his attention to the exclusion of everything else.

But today his thoughts kept going back to the woman who lived next door to him.

He couldn't understand her. She said she wanted nothing more than to run the home and look after revolving-door kids, but he knew deep down inside she must want her own family as much as he did.

She certainly had a caring heart.

And a generous smile that blessed everyone she met.

She was always touching the little guys. It was so natural and instinctive he didn't think she gave it a thought when she touched his arm or his hand when they were talking.

But he noticed. And it sent little tremors up and down his nerves.

She was a woman made for loving.

Where did that come from? Sounded like the beginning of a country ballad. He snorted. One that ended, "and she left me for another."

Perhaps it wasn't that far from reality. Laureen was totally devoted to a cause. He knew she would never see him as anything more than someone to help her with the kids.

He twitched the mouse on the mouse pad and shut down the program that by now had gone into sleep mode. Grabbing his empty coffee cup, he slammed out of the office and strode down the hall to the lunchroom.

He was thankful the room was empty. He filled his cup and

carried it to the window and leaned against the frame staring out, his mind far from the rustling trees outside.

What was she? A Mother Teresa?

The anger slipped from his shoulders, and he slumped into a chair.

Okay, admit it, man. You're attracted to the lady and bugged because she makes it clear there is no room in her life for romance.

So live with it. She's not the only fish in the pond.

Yeah, he half moaned. But the other fish often turned out to be sharks or barracudas. This was the first angelfish he'd ever meet. Or wanted to kiss.

Grinning at his comparisons and at his own stupidity in wanting what he couldn't have, he went back to the shop whistling.

❧

Laureen stood before Kyler as he cried silently, tears streaming down his face. "What's the matter?"

"My ball's stuck." He pointed to the roof.

Laureen hugged him. "We'll get it."

She looked at the roof. It was just a bungalow house with a low roof. All she needed was to get a ladder and climb up. She shivered. Not a big deal.

She dragged the ladder from the shed and heaved it against the side of the house. She made sure the extension was locked in place. She jiggled the feet of the ladder and tested its stability.

"I'll just climb up and get it."

Kyler nodded, his face screwed up with worry.

"It's not a big deal," she murmured as she placed her foot gingerly on the lower rung. Squeezing her eyes tight, she gripped the ladder with both hands and pulled herself to the next rung. "I can do this," she whispered and slowly pulled herself up rung after rung.

The roof came into view. And lots and lots of blue sky. Her throat threatened to close off so she couldn't breath.

Slowly she turned her head a fraction to the right. She saw the ball. Right there. Not more than six inches from her white-knuckled hand. But to get it would require letting go of the metal ladder.

She lifted her index finger. And ordered the next finger to let go. But she couldn't make the rest of her hand obey.

"Umph?" Kyler made anxious little sounds.

"It's okay." She looked down to reassure him.

And discovered it was a fatal error in judgment. Her head felt as if it were floating. She was so dizzy she thought she would fall. Nausea rose in her stomach, and she grabbed the ladder in a choke hold. *Please, God. Help me down.*

But she couldn't move. She was frozen to the ladder like a hot tongue on a cold piece of metal.

"Looking for something up there?"

A jolt twitched through her nerves at the sound of Pete's voice.

God, is this Your idea of a joke? I don't want him to see me stuck up here like a scared rabbit.

"Laureen?" He sounded curious. "What are you doing?"

"I'm stuck." Her voice was muffled against her arms, but she couldn't let go. Not for the life of her. Not even to keep Pete from seeing her predicament.

"Stuck? On what? A nail—?"

"On this stupid ladder." She squeezed the words out between her clenched teeth. He didn't even see the problem. How humiliating.

"You're not stuck. Just come down."

She'd never thought of Pete as dense. Until now. "I can't. I'm scared."

"Scared?"

She didn't have to see him to picture the surprised look on his face. And then he laughed.

She scowled. He had the nerve to laugh. If she weren't stuck up here, scared out of her mind, she'd kick him in the shins.

"Scared, huh? I wonder what we should do about that. Eh, Kyler. What do you think?"

If he laughed one more time, she promised she would—she turned to scowl at him and immediately regretted it. A wave of nausea left her shaking. She squeezed the ladder again.

"Just get me down."

"I suppose I could call a crane."

"Very funny," she murmured. "Do you mind?"

"Not at all. Besides you're in little danger."

She gritted her teeth. Easy for him to say.

The ladder shuddered, and she squealed.

"Calm down. I'm coming up to get you."

She clung to the ladder like a drowning man to a life raft. But the ladder shook with his ascent, and her heart squeezed so hard a pain shot through her chest.

His hands touched her ankle, and she screamed.

"Okay. I'm here. I'll keep you from falling. You can move down a rung."

But she couldn't move.

"Of course if you prefer to stay here and enjoy the view. Look at the robins over there in the elm tree. And—"

"Okay, okay."

Her jaw clenched so tight she could feel the fillings in her teeth. Inch by agonizing inch she pulled one foot off the rung and let it fall toward the lower one.

He held the ladder on either side of her body. As long as he didn't move any faster than she did, she might make it. But if his arms let go—

She shivered.

"It's okay. I won't let you fall."

She believed his soothing words and made it safely to the next step.

"There. That wasn't so bad," he murmured so close to her ear she felt his breath lift the hair at her neck. "One step at a time and we'll soon be down."

Rung by rung they descended. As soon as she stepped to terra firma, he moved back.

Her chest sank as she let out a huge gust of air. She felt the trees tip sideways.

"Whoa. Don't go passing out on me." He pulled her against his chest, and she crumpled into him.

"I'm sorry," she mumbled. This hadn't happened in a long time. Of course she avoided ladders at all costs. But other people made it look so easy. "Thanks for rescuing me."

"Glad to be of service," he said. "What are neighbors for?"

She stepped back but couldn't look at him. Not after her display of weakness. It made her want to run and hide.

He wiped a strand of hair off her cheek. "You look ready to collapse. Just rest while I take Kyler for his carving lesson."

Grateful for the chance to gather herself into a reasonable, functioning human being, she thanked him and hurried inside.

She lay on the couch, her arm draped across her forehead.

I must have looked so stupid, she moaned.

And poor Kyler. *I never did get his ball back. Or did Pete find it?* She didn't know. She'd been too wrapped up in her fear.

Groaning, she squeezed her eyes tight. What a hypocrite. She'd told Kyler how she'd overcome her fear of heights with God's help, and now she'd proven herself a liar in full blazing color.

She'd let God down.

She'd let Kyler down.

Would he ever believe anything she told him in the future?

O God, forgive me for forgetting to trust You, and help Kyler not to be adversely affected. And be with him and the Thompsons as they visit Saturday. Give them a lasting bond of love.

For a long time she lay praying. Not only for Kyler and his future but also Michael and Davey.

Please help us find a home for them.

And she prayed she would be steadfast in her commitment to these kids. A little later she went to her room and opened her Bible. After reading a few minutes, she felt refreshed. Her purpose was restored when Pete brought Kyler back.

Kyler said thanks to Pete and rushed into the house, a pleased expression on his face.

"Looks like you had a good time," Laureen said as he passed.

He nodded once, then stopped and slowly turned to face her. "I did," he said clearly and with enthusiasm before he went into the living room.

Laureen smiled after him then turned back to Pete. "Thanks."

He shrugged. "For what?"

"For helping him." Somehow Pete inspired Kyler to talk more, and for that Laureen was grateful. Just as she appreciated the time Pete spent showing Kyler how to make his wooden figures.

"What are you planning to do on Saturday?" Pete asked. "Didn't you say Kyler would be gone all afternoon?"

๛

Laureen sat beside Pete on the front seat of his four-by-four as he turned into the parking lot and drove down the row of cars looking for a spot close to the gate.

She had agreed to come with him solely because it was preferable to staying home alone. The house had been ghostly silent after the Thompsons picked up Kyler, promising to have him back by nine.

Pete found a spot and turned off the motor. With the air conditioner suddenly quiet, heat filled the cab. He reached behind the seat and pulled out a folded window cardboard and stuck it in place to block the window.

By the time he was finished, Laureen was standing under the shade of the trees.

"Nice picture." She tipped her head toward the cardboard in the window where a tiger snarled.

"Thanks. I like it. Got your hat and sunglasses and sunscreen?" Pete asked before he locked the vehicle.

"Yup. It's all here." She patted the big straw shoulder bag. "That and wipes, tissues, bandages, a spare pair of shades, a—"

He held up his hands in surrender. "You sound like my mother. You'd almost think you were used to traveling with children."

She wrinkled her nose and tried to look offended. "Your mother, indeed! And here I thought I was only being a good Scout."

"What's the motto? Be prepared?" He took her hand and pulled her toward the gate. "Let's see how prepared you are then."

She giggled at the challenge in his voice. She was prepared for minor incidents like a sliver or ice cream all over a little face. But she wasn't prepared for the way her heart felt all jittery. As if she'd taken the last step too soon and her foot had found nothing but air. It wasn't a scary feeling. More like an unexpected thrill.

Pete read the sign at the gate. " 'Free Park.' Bet they wished they'd given it a different name, because with a name like that they don't dare charge admission."

"Isn't that why it's so named?" Laureen tipped her head. She hadn't thought of it before. She'd just been grateful she had a cheap place to take the kids. And lots of free things to do if one chose.

Pete looked shocked. "You mean you haven't heard the history of our fair town?"

"Well, some, I guess." After all she'd had to supervise homework, and part of the curriculum included local history.

"Freetown is named after an early family—Mr. and Mrs. Free." Still holding her hand, he led her through the gate and along the sidewalk.

She nodded. That much she knew.

"This park"—he waved his hand in an encompassing gesture—"is part of their original holdings. Come—I'll show you where it all started."

He led her down a wide, dusty road. She'd never been this way before. It was the opposite direction from the playground area. "This is the original house." It was an old two-story farmhouse with flower boxes full of red geraniums and white lace curtains at the windows. "It's been restored." They went inside. Pete crossed his arms, still holding Laureen's hand securely. Her hand rested against his chest. This wasn't what she'd bargained for. No sirree. This afternoon's outing was supposed to be a diversion while Kyler was away. Nothing more.

She'd had a long talk with herself last night about what she would and would not allow to develop between her and Pete. And she and herself had come to a complete understanding. Friendship was in. Romance was out.

Trouble was—he seemed oblivious to the quandary his claim of her hand put her in as he led her through the house, commenting on various items and explaining the history of the Free family.

Back outside he let his arms drop to his sides, her hand still held securely in his warm grasp.

Apart from jerking away rudely, Laureen seemed to have no option but to let him hold her hand.

It's just a casual gesture of friendship, she told herself. *Yeah, right. Maybe in his mind.* But the close contact made it difficult for Laureen to keep her attention on what Pete was saying about the barn.

"Mrs. Free was a devoted gardener so she had developed much of this original park area." Pete pointed out the corners of the original yard.

Laureen had no intention of letting things get out of hand. *Remember our little talk,* she told herself.

But it was the memory of her time of prayer that snapped her back to reality. She'd renewed her commitment to obeying God's call on her heart to work with displaced children.

"The Frees had no children," Pete continued. "So when Mrs. Free died she willed all this land to the town with the provision it remain a park in perpetuity." He had guided them toward a gazebo almost hidden beneath purple flowering clematis at the end of a sidewalk. "I understand she had the first gazebo built here on this very site though it's been re-placed over the years."

"It's lovely." On the pretext of wanting to run ahead and examine the flowers, she pulled her hand away.

Pete followed more slowly and leaned against one of the pillars. His smile tilted to one side as he watched her.

Laureen wondered if he guessed why she had hurried away.

She circled the inside of the gazebo. "It's lovely." The climbing vines made for a pleasant setting. When Pete stepped inside, his eyes dark, his gaze searching hers, she realized how intimate the setting was and hurried out the far side.

Pete ambled after her, the creases in his cheeks deepening as if he were amused.

She knew her flight away from him had not gone unnoticed.

They toured the rest of Mrs. Free's gardens. At the end of the path Pete paused. "How about a game of minigolf?"

Laureen grinned. A game was more in her line. "You're on." She took off running. "Race ya."

"Cheat."

His steps thundered after her.

six

She was seized by giggles and half stumbled.

He caught up to her and ran past, jeering, "Cheaters never prosper." Then he jogged around her and grabbed her elbow. "Come on, gal. No time to loiter. I'm going to show you how to play a wicked game of minigolf."

She chortled. "You forget I was raised with two brothers." She paused for effect. "Two competitive brothers."

"Ooh. Sounds like a challenge. I'm so scared."

She lifted her chin and marched to the booth and bought tickets for them both. When Pete tried to edge his way in to pay, she waved him aside. "My pleasure." She grabbed the putter and plopped the ball on the first tee. "Just like it will be my pleasure to show you who's the better man in golf." She whacked the ball down the green strip of indoor-outdoor carpeting. The ball rolled neatly through the opening and bounced around the first corner. She perched her club over her shoulder and faced Pete. "Prepare to be soundly beaten, Mr. Long."

"Hah. It ain't over 'til the fat lady sings."

He whacked his ball so hard it bounced right off the course and he had to take another turn.

"Hah, yourself," she jeered. "Better get the fat lady ready."

She played consistently well while he played erratically, sometimes playing a good shot, but just as often wasting his play. But it didn't seem to matter. He laughed and joked as if he were far in the lead. And she gloated over every victory. By the time they got to the end she was miles ahead. She stood at attention, placed her hand on her chest, and began singing, "O Canada, our home and native land—"

He grabbed her hand and practically dragged her away.

"What's the matter?" she sputtered. "Aren't I fat enough?"

He laughed so hard she thought he was going to break something. After glowering at him for all of five seconds she laughed equally hard.

They collapsed on a park bench to catch their breath.

ða

Pete couldn't remember when he'd had more fun. He smiled so hard his cheeks hurt. And his stomach ached from laughing. Laureen was one of the best sports he'd ever met. It was as if she thought everything was intended for her very own enjoyment.

From a completely crazy round of minigolf in which she had whomped him fair and square, a fact she refused to let him forget, they had gone to the lake and rented paddle boats. She splashed and teased and goofed around until they were both soaking wet and weak with laughter.

She was like a hummingbird flitting from one amusing bit of nonsense to another. He wanted to catch her in his hand and hold her gently as he would a small bird. He reached for her, but she spun around to comment on a yellow-headed black bird perched on a reed. They were on a boardwalk over a swampy area. The air was filled with the chatter of marsh birds.

She straightened and grinned at him. "Have you ever seen so many birds in one spot?"

He shook his head and leaned against the railing. "Noisy

little suckers, aren't they?" He watched her, aching to get closer. Yesterday, helping her off the ladder and then holding her so she wouldn't faint at his feet, had made him realize how fond he'd grown of her. But it was a no-win situation. She was devoted to the home kids. He doubted she would ever have room in her life for a normal home and family.

She turned her back to the birds and leaned on the railing. "This is a wonderful place. So quiet." She chuckled. "I can just see me bringing a pack of boys here. They'd enjoy pounding up and down the sidewalk. There wouldn't be a bird left within shouting distance. We'd probably be asked to leave the park. Permanently."

He swallowed hard. Her hand was barely an inch away from his. He'd noticed how she'd shied away more than once this afternoon as if uncomfortable with holding hands. Had she changed her mind? Was this an invitation?

He didn't need much of an invitation. He slid his hand over until the sides of their palms touched. His pulse echoed in the stillness inside his head when she didn't jerk away. Instead she turned her palm upward into his fingers. Her hand was soft and warm.

"I hear they have a nice snack bar next to the playground," he said. Keeping her hand in his, he headed toward the area wishing for a restaurant with candlelight and soft music about five steps away.

When they got to the food booth he saw a sign that interested him. PICNIC BASKETS PREPARED HERE.

He ordered one complete with sandwiches of choice and tiny pastries. Ham and cheese for him, egg salad for Laureen. No choice on the pastries, but cherry tarts and bite-sized brownies looked more than adequate. The lady packed it into a wicker basket containing a pair of red plates, two white glasses, red-checked napkins, and matching tablecloth. She handed it to Pete.

"Have a good time." She winked.

Pete grinned at her and took the basket. He fully intended to follow her instructions.

Laureen helped him carry the basket to a grassy spot under a large weeping birch.

He looked around. Perfect. Secluded yet not so much as to scare her. Already she had the basket open and was spreading the square tablecloth. He knelt beside her and helped arrange the food on the cloth.

Then with their backs to the tree they bit into the sandwiches.

"Umm, good," Laureen said. "I didn't realize how hungry I was."

"Me, too."

She seemed as content as he to stay there, watching the people come and go.

The sky had clouded over enough to make it only pleasantly warm. They sat on the eastern side of a tall stand of pine trees so the shadows put them into a kind of semigloom that made Pete feel as if they were all alone.

They seemed to have no need for conversation. They watched a woman and her brood of six screaming kids order burgers and pop. Pete noticed the mother look around, eyeing a picnic table about thirty feet from where her bunch inhaled burgers. Then her shoulders rose and fell, and she turned back to them.

He chuckled. "Poor lady."

Laureen nodded. "Doesn't it make you want to go over there and help her?"

He shuddered. "Oh, yeah. About as much as I'd like to have a root canal."

"I wonder how Kyler's day is going?"

Pete had forgotten the little boy. This was a big day for him. "What time will he be back?"

"Nine."

It was seven now. "I suppose we should start back." His plans included lingering in the original part of the park.

They packed up the picnic things and returned them to the booth then wandered back toward the entrance.

Pete directed their path, and when they had a choice of going through the playground area or back through the flower gardens, he led them toward the flowers.

The fragrance of stocks and petunias filled the air. Laureen seemed content to hold hands. He chose the sidewalk leading back to the gazebo. She allowed him to lead her up the four steps and into the shadowed interior without a word.

He stopped dead center and inhaled the scent of flowers. It was enough to make his head swim. "It's been a real nice day."

She smiled up at him. "A wonderful day. Thanks for showing me a little bit of Freetown history." A huge sigh lifted her shoulders, and then she straightened. "It's time for me to go home."

seven

Kyler had returned shortly after she'd said a hurried good-bye to Pete. The Thompsons said they'd been happy enough with the visit though admittedly disappointed that Kyler said nothing until he got back home, and then his "thank you" was at Laureen's gentle insistence.

They seemed to understand, though, how he'd feel uneasy around them—this being their first outing. But they were eager to proceed, and a schedule of visits was set up.

"Is there any chance we could have him by September?" Ann Thompson had asked. "In time for him to start school? It would save his having to be moved and all."

Laureen appreciated her eagerness. "If things go well, it might be possible." Less than six weeks. She pressed her lips together to hide her emotions. She was happy for him. She was. But she was sad at the thought of losing him.

Kyler had been cooperative about going to bed. Through the monitor she heard little mumblings from his room and could picture him lining up tiny cars on his bed or talking to the three little pieces of wood—the Woodknot family. It was his way of sorting out things. She hoped he would someday feel free to talk to his new family, but she guessed he would always prefer to sort things through in his head. It wasn't such a bad way to be.

If only she could do the same.

She stood in the middle of her room and looked around.

This was her retreat every bit as much as Kyler's room was his.

She had surrounded herself with comforting things: her desk and journal, her china cat with its pleased expression. It always made her feel better when she saw it. On the opposite corner of the desk was a framed picture of her and her family taken two years ago when they had all gotten together for a weekend.

Over the desk hung her favorite poster—a cartoon cat, clinging to a rope by one claw. Underneath was the caption "When you get to the end of your rope, let go. Underneath are the everlasting arms." And beneath the caption a cupped pair of hands.

Right now she was feeling like that frazzled cat.

Her reactions this afternoon had surprised her. She'd accepted that she would likely live a single life, and it had never mattered before. Now, suddenly, she felt attracted to other things. Namely Pete. Did she want more than friendship from their relationship?

She retreated to the big armchair beside the bed, pausing to smooth a corner of the burgundy-and-green-plaid bedspread. From the nearby bookcase, overflowing with books and CDs, she took her Bible and curled up. Her gaze rested on the framed crewel picture she'd made her first year of university. That was the year she'd wondered if she was seeking only her own glory in her career choice as one of her classmates had suggested. And choosing a less demanding route was tempting. Especially when so many things appealed to her. And most especially appealing was a certain young man with whom she'd enjoyed many pleasant evenings. Gordon. Gordon James Brier with beautiful blue eyes and thick curly blond hair. He had seemed fine in both character and looks.

Now as she remembered him he seemed a bit weak. And he had wanted things that didn't fit with her view of Christian ideals. When she'd said she wanted to devote herself to helping kids, he had accused her of being a Protestant nun, and that was the last she saw of him. Working on this picture had helped her become centered again. "Life is fragile—handle with prayer," it said, the words surrounded by a bouquet of flowers over which hovered a hummingbird.

That was her answer. She would pray until her thoughts cleared.

Lord God, You know my heart better than I do. You understand my confusion. I want to be obedient to the call You have placed on my life in caring for these kids. I always thought that meant there would never be a place for anything but friendship between me and a man. But my feelings toward Pete are more than that. I know it. And I don't know what to do about it.

She sat quietly, waiting for peace to fill her. After a few minutes, feeling the need for specific direction, she opened the Bible to a familiar passage: Psalm 119. She started at the beginning. At verse 5 she stopped and reread the verse: "Oh, that my ways were steadfast in obeying your decrees!"

She read it again then bowed her head. *Thank You, Lord. Above all I want to be obedient.*

With obedience as her guiding principle she allowed herself to think about her relationship with Pete. She truly liked him in a way she'd never cared for another man. She might even, she admitted, love him just a tiny bit. But whether or not she could give him her heart depended on a lot of things. His feelings about her, to start with. From his actions this afternoon it seemed he might be at least fond of her, but until he said how he felt she could only guess.

Then there was her work. Could she combine marriage and work? Did she want to? Would Pete be agreeable? It was the first time she'd considered combining work and marriage. Now suddenly it seemed so practical and sensible. Why hadn't she thought of the idea before?

Because—she sank back into the chair, her Bible clutched to her chest, a dreamy smile widening her mouth—because she'd never known a man who made her want such an arrangement.

But she was getting way ahead of herself. These were all things that could be discussed and resolved as their relationship grew.

Perhaps things would work out. But she was prepared to take her time.

❧

Michael and Davey returned after lunch the next day. The first thing Michael did was sweep his arm across the picnic table where Kyler had his trucks and cars lined up in precise order and knock them all flying.

"Michael." Laureen stood in front of him, but Michael refused to meet her look. "You can't behave like that."

"I didn't do nothing." He sidestepped her.

She sighed. It looked as if the boys had had a fun time at camp. But did the counselors?

"Come on, Diddly Bum," Michael ordered Davey.

Davey jumped to obey, but Laureen intervened. "Michael, we aren't allowed to talk to people like that around here."

He glowered at her. "Like what?"

She squared her shoulders. This kid was back to the belligerence they had worked on for the past four months. "Like calling people names as you just did."

"Diddly Bum ain't a name. That's what he is." He faced Davey. "Diddly Bum Davey."

"Davey, Kyler, you come inside." She grabbed Michael's shoulder and hung on, knowing he would try to escape. "Michael, you are having a time out."

He squirmed all the way to the door, then sullenly allowed her to steer him to his bedroom. He lay on the bed while she sat on a chair in the hall to make sure he remained in his room. Some people simply set a timer. Ten minutes and you're done. Laureen preferred to let them choose how long they stayed there. Her rule was they could come out as soon as they were prepared to behave or offer an apology or whatever was needed.

The only trouble was, at least two staff members were usually on duty so one could stay with the time-out boy while the other supervised the rest of the boys.

Davey came in and, after giving her a dark look, flitted away to his room.

Kyler stood in the kitchen doorway, a worried look on his face.

"You go get your cars and trucks, and you can play with them on the kitchen table."

He nodded and slipped outside to retrieve them. Back inside he sat where he could see her.

Poor little guy. His safe, quiet world has been shaken.

Something must have shaken Michael's world, too.

Lord, I don't know what happened at camp to upset Michael. I'll really need Your wisdom to keep things in line, though.

From the next bedroom came thumping sounds. Davey banging his head. If Michael had a bad time, Davey had a bad time.

Kyler made soft noises in the kitchen, playing with his Woodknot family.

Laureen checked Michael. He rolled on his side and stubbornly kept his face to the wall. She leaned back and rested her head against the wall. It looked as if she was in for a long sit. She could scoop up a book from the living room, but she didn't feel like reading.

She'd seen Pete only briefly at church that morning. She'd slipped in late. The service had gone on overtime. Yet even though she had to hurry away to be back for the boys' return, she'd waited to speak to him.

"Will I see you later?" he'd asked when she explained her hurry.

She nodded. "I should be free about four or five. Marj is due back then."

"Could we go for coffee? We need to talk."

She'd nodded agreement to both the invitation for coffee and the need to talk. She had so many things she wanted to ask him. Would he sense the difference in her? It was so freeing to know she'd decided to accept his friendship, and more, if she was certain it didn't interfere with what she understood God wanted from her. She wondered if it showed in her face, her expression, her words.

But she hadn't anticipated the change in Michael and Davey's behavior.

They had been doing so well. Now she worried she might not be able to leave Marj with the three of them.

She glanced at Michael again. His chest rose slowly and steadily. Wondering, she tiptoed over. He had fallen asleep. The thumping in the next room had ended. She glanced in. Davey lay spread-eagled, his mouth open. He, too, slept.

Maybe all they needed was to catch up on their sleep.

Kyler played happily in the kitchen so Laureen made a pot of coffee. As it spurted through the filter, she wished Pete could share a cup with her. She wanted someone to talk to. Not just someone, she amended. She wanted to share her concerns with Pete.

She smiled as she poured her coffee. She'd never been one to want sympathy or understanding from another. If things got crazy, she'd either go to her room and sit quietly, praying and reading her Bible, or perhaps go for a walk. Once in a while she would express concerns about her own reactions at a staff meeting and let the others give suggestions and support, but now she ached for a different sort of concern.

She opened up the Sunday paper as she sat across from Kyler.

Half an hour later she heard a dreadful crash down the hall. Laureen rushed to Michael's bedroom to find him slamming his closet door.

She shook her head. "Come on, Michael. Let's go have some cookies and milk." He looked as if he might throw something at her instead; then glowering thunderously he stomped toward the kitchen.

The commotion had wakened Davey, and he let out a muffled cry then swallowed his tears and joined them for a snack.

Laureen studied the pair. Dark circles under their eyes. She hugged each boy to her side. "What was the best thing about camp?"

Davey shrugged. Michael glowered.

It looked as if they were set for some serious one-on-one talks and some structured playtime. She hoped she could get them to verbalize what had gone wrong. They would have to work on appropriate ways of expressing displeasure. It had been months since they'd had to channel anger physically with Michael.

An hour later Marj walked in the door, calling a greeting to everyone. When Michael practically growled at her, Marj's eyes widened. She glanced at Laureen.

Laureen gave a weary nod. "They got back from camp this afternoon. I don't know if they're just tired or if they had a bad time."

Marj grinned. "Missed us, didn't you, boys?"

"What's to miss?" Michael snarled. "This is a stupid place." He pushed Davey off his chair and, his fists swinging, leaned over his little brother.

Laureen grabbed Michael before he could land a punch and wrapped her arms around him in a gentle restraint. Marj pulled Davey to his feet and patted his back.

Out of the corner of her eye Laureen could see Kyler withdrawing into himself. Who could blame him? The peace they had enjoyed for two weeks had been shattered as if by an earthquake.

Marj shepherded the two younger boys to the living room.

Laureen held Michael until he stopped struggling; then she turned him about to face him. "Michael, what's bothering you?"

"Nothin'."

"Nothing happened at camp to upset you?"

"Camp was stupid."

"So you're glad to be home again?"

"This place is stupid."

Laureen sighed. "I wish I knew what your problem is." She hoped Michael would meet her eyes, but he stared past her shoulder, his expression dark and angry. She'd wanted to tease him and tell him he had a bad case of "stupids," but Michael was certainly not in a mood for teasing. "Maybe you're just tired." She heard the TV in the other room and led him to a big armchair a safe distance from the other two boys who huddled on the couch watching him warily.

She and Marj slipped away, hovering near the door where they talked quietly while keeping an eye on the boys.

"Any idea what's wrong with Michael?"

"No, I'm hoping he'll say something to give us a clue. But, hey, you have to hear about the good stuff that happened while you were away."

Hugging Marj's arm, she told how Kyler had started talking. "And Pete offered to help him carve some figures for the fall fair."

"Wow. Double wow. I want to hear him talk."

Laureen slipped over to the couch and whispered for Kyler to come with her. When they were in the safe quiet of the kitchen, she bent over and took his face between her hands, wishing she could do something to erase the wariness she saw there. Poor kid. No doubt he wondered if Michael's anger would be turned on him.

"Tell Marj what you and Pete are doing."

Kyler's eyes widened. His gaze darted from Laureen's face to Marj and back again in a nervous dance.

"I'd really like to know," Marj urged softly.

But rather than open his mouth Kyler dug in his pocket and pulled out his Woodknot family. Giving them a loving look, he held them out to Marj.

"This is what you and Pete are doing?" Marj asked.

He nodded several times, then paused. Laureen could see

the confusion in his eyes. Finally he shook his head.

"Can you tell Marj about the family figures you're carving?" Laureen encouraged him.

He shook his head again.

"Maybe later," Marj said. "Kyler, you stay right there. I have something for you." She hurried to the office and returned with a package.

Kyler opened it slowly and pulled out a set of six miniature trucks. A smile spread across his face.

"Can you say thank you to Marj?" Laureen asked softly, praying he would do so.

He looked at Marj and nodded then pointed toward his bedroom and gave Laureen a questioning look.

She straightened. "Yes, you can go to your room to play."

"Maybe later," Marj said after he'd left.

Laureen nodded. "I hope so. I better get some supper made for them." She prepared a stack of grilled cheese sandwiches and opened a bag of chips.

Through the window she saw Pete enter the backyard and checked the clock. She'd forgotten the time. She darted a glance at the plates with their steaming sandwiches, the cheese oozing out in soft rolls, then stared at the door, unable to move. It was the first time she could remember feeling as if she wanted to be in two places at once.

Marj came from the other room. "Company?"

"I told Pete I would go out for coffee with him." She shrugged. "I didn't know things would be so complicated with the boys returning."

Marj's eyes widened at the news, and then she moved to open the door. "I think I can manage the boys. They seem to be content to watch the movie. You go ahead. You can use the break. Pete, eh? Good work."

She opened the door, and Pete strode in. He greeted Marj, then turned toward Laureen, giving her one of those slow, dimple-deepening smiles that turned Laureen's insides as warm and mushy as the melted cheese.

Again she felt pulled in two directions. She turned to Marj, but before she could voice her uncertainty about going out Marj spoke.

"Tomorrow we can go over news and plans." She waved her arms. "Shoo. Away you go and enjoy yourself. I'll get the boys into bed so don't worry about hurrying back." And with that she disappeared into the living room carrying the sandwich plates.

Laureen met Pete's eyes. Mentally she clung to his gaze, letting herself swim in his kindness and concern.

"Are you comfortable with leaving her?" he asked. "If you're not, we can cancel or do something else. It's okay with me."

His words were all it took for Laureen to make up her mind. "No, I really do want to get away." She glanced down at her stained T-shirt. "Just give me a minute to change."

☙

Pete studied the woman across the table from him. The rays of late afternoon sun slanted through the window catching the prisms on the chandelier, throwing rainbow shards across the room. One patch of color danced in the dark strands of Laureen's hair as she studied the plate of tea sandwiches in front of her.

She had been subdued on the walk to the historic Dr. Kent house, which was now a quiet tea shop.

"Something on your mind?" he asked.

She glanced up and gave him a crooked smile that went

straight to his heart. "Yes. I guess there is." He wanted to reach over with both hands cupped and tell her to put all her troubles right there: He'd take care of them for her. It was a feeling so unexpected and so far from what he'd decided that it felt as if he'd landed on his feet after a long fall, taking his breath from him and leaving his lungs aching for relief.

She told him how Michael and Davey had returned, upset and out of sorts. "Maybe I shouldn't have sent them to camp."

"You can't blame yourself."

"I don't." Her smile widened, making his insides dance. "Okay, maybe I do. I don't like feeling powerless." Her smile faded, leaving him anxious. "I admit it is sometimes pretty discouraging."

He studied her. Was she having doubts about her work? Was she—? He could hardly swallow. Was she wondering if she wanted to keep doing this year after year? Had their time together given her a desire for something less draining, more satisfying? Like being a wife and mother? *My wife. The mother of my children.*

He'd spent a long time thinking and praying last night after their day in the park. He valued her friendship, but he wasn't prepared to give his heart to someone who had set her sights on something else.

But with her facing him across the table, with her blue eyes dark and troubled, all he could think was. . .maybe. Maybe she'd change her mind. Maybe there would be room in her heart for a family of her own.

"Have you thought about doing something else with your life?" *Like marriage and family?* he silently added. *Pick me. Pick me,* he wanted to shout.

She grew so still he thought she must be holding her breath.

"Quit, you mean?" But she didn't wait for him to answer. "I'm sorry. I didn't mean to give the impression I wanted to give up." Her expression grew fierce. "I can't imagine ever giving up on a child."

Disappointment snaked through his heart. Back to square one. But square one held no appeal. "You've never had a failure? A child you had to give up on?"

"How do you measure success or failure? It's so often three steps forward and two steps back." She gave a quick laugh. "Sometimes it feels as if the forward steps are baby-sized and the backward ones are giant steps; but, to date, all our boys have been placed in homes. The families to which they've gone have had extensive counseling and training. But frankly I seldom hear from them or about them after they leave unless they return—and some have. I suppose you could call that a failure." She gave him an impish grin. "I prefer to call it a need for reassessment."

He laughed. "Sounds politically correct." The waitress slipped into the little room where they sat alone and removed their plates. He'd hardly noticed what he'd eaten. Trying to direct his thoughts away from the woman across the table so he could think rationally, he glanced around the room, taking in the wood flooring and woodwork that had been restored to gleaming warmth. Fine workmanship. And nice job of making the place look and feel old-fashioned and genteel. He rubbed his fingers along the hem of the white cloth napkin. No paper or plastic in the place. Soft music filtered through the room. In the hall a ceiling fan hummed quietly.

He completed a visual tour of the room, and his gaze returned to Laureen. She wore a wide-necked white dress that made her look as fresh as morning sunlight.

The waitress slid a plate of strawberry shortcake in front of each of them.

He took a forkful. The sweet strawberries, mellow whipped cream, and melt-in-your-mouth biscuits gave him something else to think about for a few minutes.

"You wanted to talk about something?" Laureen asked.

"It can wait until we're done."

"I won't be able to bring Kyler over as often now that the others are back."

Did he detect regret in her voice? "Bring him when you can." How much were things going to change? He'd have to be honest with himself. He hadn't anticipated this, and suddenly he realized how much he'd miss those evening visits.

"It won't be the same, I'm afraid," she said.

He looked deep into her eyes, which held his gaze with that unblinking directness he had come to expect. He read her thoughts in her eyes and knew she would miss their times as much as he. It gave him hope. But he needed to clear up some things between them. He pushed away from the table. "Let's take a walk."

They left the historic house and walked past the older homes of Freetown.

"I love this part of town." Laureen paused at a yard sheltered by tall trees. "All the mature trees and big old houses. Do you ever wonder about the people who planted those?"

From out of nowhere a huge German shepherd roared toward them, barking and growling, tackling the fence.

Pete grabbed Laureen around the shoulders and dragged her away from the fence. "Moving right along," he murmured, pulling her along until they were safely away from the dog. He'd had visions of the dog tearing her flesh into strips. It shook him more than he wanted to admit.

Laureen stopped, stepping away from him, her hand pressed to her chest. "That scared me half to death." She laughed. "We'd better be careful."

"Careful. How?"

She grew serious. "What would happen if I'm scared half to death twice? Two halves are a whole, right? It could be really serious."

Slow amusement spread through him, and he laughed. "You're crazy."

"Only way to be."

They fell in step again and rounded a corner.

"Look! A playground." She pointed to the swings and slide hidden behind dusty, tall pine trees. "Come on. Let's play." She ran to the swings and plunked down.

Pete watched her. She'd gone from worrying about the home to all fun and games. Had she forgotten her discouragement? Or did she have the ability to put it aside for the moment? He thought he'd sorted out his feelings for her, but she was like a dancing bit of magic. As full of sweetness as a breeze from a rose garden, warm like the kiss of the summer sun.

"Come on, Pete. Give me a push."

"Okay." He moved behind her to do as she requested.

eight

Laureen loved his company. He made her feel protected and cherished rather than the person who always had to be controlling things. It would be pleasant to have that sort of refuge at the end of each day. And if he accepted her commitment to her job and the kids. . .

Perhaps God had brought them together for that reason. To give her someone for her.

She chided herself. That sounded so selfish. God was enough. He was her rock and her fortress.

But it would be nice to share her concerns with someone. After all, even God had said it wasn't good for man to be alone. Sometimes it wasn't so good for a woman, either.

She slipped from the swing and stood facing him. Neither of them moved.

The only sound came from the birds visiting in the nearby trees. She waited, wondering if he felt the possibilities as much as she did.

But he only reached for her hand. "Let's walk some more."

They continued touring the streets of old Freetown. Laureen pointed out a flash as a blue jay darted between the branches of a dusty evergreen, the newly painted gingerbread trim on a house, the exuberant purple on another house, the thread of music from someone playing a piano, the heady scent of petunias as they breathed into the late hours of the day.

Pete laughed at her comments and squeezed her hand

when she recalled events from her childhood. They paused beneath a thick overhang of pine boughs to study a little picture book abandoned there.

As he bent over the pages, she studied his face. In the dusky shadows his expression was cloaked.

He looked up and caught her staring.

"Laureen? What is it?"

She shook her head. "I was just thinking."

"About me? About us?"

"Maybe."

"Is there a maybe?"

Did he sound hopeful? Could she believe he had thought about them? "I don't know."

He tilted his head, and a finger of sunlight caught his dark eyes, revealing an expression she thought disclosed hesitation.

"I admit I enjoy your company," she said, her voice slow and uncertain. It wasn't what she wanted to say. She wanted to tell him how she yearned for him to understand her quandary—committed to her job yet longing for something more—maybe even a home of her own. It was an entirely new dilemma for her. Never before had she even considered she might need, or even want, a life apart from working with kids.

She forced herself to be lighthearted. "You're such a good sport about being whipped in minigolf."

"I let you win." His smile deepened the corners of his mouth.

"Yeah, I believe that."

He sobered. "Laureen, what happens when the workers at the home marry? Are they required to leave?"

"No. They can still work if they want to." Her words sounded breathy. Was he wondering if they could work out something? "Some have married and stayed on staff." They didn't seem to stay long, but maybe they had their own reasons for moving on.

He didn't make any further comment, just pulled her arm through his and led her home, taking the long scenic route.

In her bedroom she curled up in the comfort of the armchair and thought about the evening.

God, are You bringing us together? Give me wisdom to know what to do. To know Your will.

She had responsibilities, and until she knew how he felt and what that meant in terms of her future here at the home she would hold herself in check. Despite her attraction to him she would not let her emotions control her. It was as she'd said to Pete more than once; she could never imagine abandoning a child. Her first loyalty belonged to the kids in her care.

If a man were ever to be in her life, she'd have to trust God to work it out so she could combine both marriage and her job.

And please, God, if it be Your will, let it work out with Pete.

For she knew she cared for Pete in a way she had never expected to experience.

❧

Late the next afternoon the doorbell rang, and Laureen opened the door to a man and a woman.

The woman introduced herself as the mother of Michael and Davey and demanded to see them.

Called in, the boys sat facing her, looking guarded and suspicious.

"This is your new father, boys." She introduced the big man at her side. "We's married and want you to come live with us." Her dark glance at Laureen dared anyone to argue.

"You'll have to go through the proper channels," Laureen

said. "I'm sure you know all that."

"I already seen the head honcho and started the paper works. He said I should visit the boys a few times."

Laureen ventured a silent guess he'd suggested a lot more than that. Like at least phoning in advance to arrange her visit. Unwilling to let the mother have an unsupervised visit until she'd received the go ahead, Laureen remained in the room as the woman told the boys about the lumber mill her new husband owned and how much fun they'd all have together. Laureen watched the boys' response and knew from their stoic expressions they accepted the inevitable. But it was the new "daddy" she watched the closest. She didn't like the way he checked the boys out with his silent gaze, as if measuring them—either for their potential for work, Laureen guessed, or perhaps estimating how long before they would stand up to him.

She didn't like what she saw, but unless something horrible happened to prove her suspicions, she knew the boys would be returned to their mother. And whatever the new stepfather decided to dish out.

All she could do was pray and try to prepare the boys so they would know they could phone a number of different places if they were ever in trouble.

But it upset her so much that she kept glancing toward Pete's house, waiting for him to get home. She badly needed to talk to him and get some comfort and reassurance.

Supper simmered on the stove when she heard his truck door slam.

"Marj," she called. "Do you mind keeping an eye on the boys while I run next door and arrange Kyler's next visit?"

"No problem."

Laureen thanked her and hurried out the back gate. By the time she got there, Pete had gone inside.

He opened to her knock and gave her one of those slow, deep smiles she loved.

"Hi." His voice rumbled through her senses. "What's the problem?"

"Am I that obvious?"

His grin widened. "It's plain as that pretty little nose on your face."

She wrinkled her nose. "And the first thing I do is come running to you for sympathy?"

"That's what friends are for."

Friends? Was it enough? She didn't know.

"You're right, of course. I am upset. Well, actually, worried is a better word for how I feel." She told him about the arrival of Michael and Davey's mother and new stepfather.

"I don't like the situation."

"It certainly seems full of all sorts of land mines. It's not a good way for the adults to start a new marriage and hope for success." He pulled her toward the table and she sat down.

It wasn't the marriage that concerned her as much as the safety of the two little boys, but before she could voice her protest he continued.

"And a marriage under stress is not a good environment for children. So it seems to me the best thing you and everyone can do is make sure they're given lots of support and preparation."

"That's the problem, isn't it? What we feel is best for everyone isn't necessarily acceptable to those people. I certainly got the impression neither the mom nor the stepdad has any use for help from others." She shook her head. "All I can do is pray things work out and especially that the boys are safe."

"For sure." He reached across the table and took her hands. "No time like the present."

Seeing he meant to pray here and now, Laureen bowed her head.

"Lord God, You know this situation and what is needed. Be the protector and counselor for this family." He squeezed Laureen's hands between his and added, "And give Laureen peace and direction."

His prayer settled around her like a benediction. She kept her head bowed several seconds after he finished, letting his words of blessing fill her with peace. "Thank you," she whispered, meeting his gaze.

"For what? I only did what anyone would do."

"Maybe, maybe not." *Thank you for being such a nice man,* she answered silently. "You know this is the first time I've been inside your house since the Bowmans moved out." She looked around. "Are you sure this is the same place? I remember it as small and dark and dingy."

He pulled her to her feet. "Come—I'll give you the real estate tour. First, note the lovely dining nook."

"It's beautiful. Full of light and airiness. Almost feels as if you're outside. But"—she shook her head—"did you build it on?"

"Nope." His wide grin revealed his pleasure in her observations. "Just got rid of the big old cabinet they'd covered the windows with and took down the heavy curtains."

He led her to the living room. "I don't know if you realize it, but this is the only house that hasn't burned down in this block. So your house and the rest are about thirty years old. This one is almost a hundred. I'm trying to restore it to its original beauty while adding light and efficiency. In this room"—he stood in the center of the room Laureen remembered being as crowded and dark as the kitchen—"I've removed a false ceiling to give it more height and again taken down the heavy drapes. I'm planning to restore the wood floor this winter."

He showed her the two bedrooms, where he had built closets, and a smaller room, formerly a storage area, now converted into an office with bookshelves along one wall and against the other, a wide desk, complete with computer and printer.

"The bathroom is another project for the fall or winter. I'm going to put in new fixtures and add lots of lights."

They returned to the kitchen. Bright oak cabinetry and the off-white walls transformed the room. "I like what you're doing. It's so refreshing." She turned full circle. "This room always made me depressed. It was so crowded I felt pressed in." She could imagine a few little touches here and there to soften the room. Maybe a basket in one corner overflowing with dried flowers and grains to emphasize the new airiness. "What did you do with the washer and dryer that were there?"

Curling his finger, he motioned her past the dining nook to a second door. The room, once a cold, unwelcoming porch filled with the Bowmans' unused items, was now a sun-filled laundry room.

"Off the kitchen like this," Pete said, "is ideal. Saves a lot of steps. I'm hoping it will be a selling feature, especially for an older couple."

Laureen thought someone had sucked the air from the room. But the door was open letting in plenty of fresh air. And Pete breathed in and out normally.

"Sell? You're planning to move?"

"I won't stay here forever. I like to renovate homes and resell them. I see this house as a starter home for a young couple or a downsize home for the empty nesters."

She stared at the wall. If he sold the house and moved she wouldn't be able to see him. Nor would she be able to dream of marrying him and living next door to her work.

❧

Pete saw the shock on her face and felt himself being dragged into her worry. It gladdened him to see her reaction—as if the thought of his moving was an unwelcome notion. But he couldn't stand the way the light had gone from her eyes. He gently took her hand and pulled her back into the kitchen, pausing where they could see into the living room as well. "Would you enjoy having a home like this?"

Her gaze circled the rooms and came back to him. "Yes, I'm sure I would."

"And a family of your own to live in the house?"

Laureen's eyes developed a depth that drew him in. It was like swimming in warm heavy water that held him floating on its surface.

"Isn't that what most of us dream about?" she answered.

"Wouldn't it be nice to pour your love into your own children rather than a continual stream of kids moving in and out of the home?" Dare he hope?

Her eyes darkened, taking Pete farther into the depths. Together, he sensed, they were exploring unfamiliar territory.

"I think about it," she admitted, her eyes so blue and deep he knew he was drowning and welcomed it.

"With me?" His lungs refused to expand.

She nodded. "Yes, with you." Her words were barely a whisper.

He cupped his palm around her chin and lifted her face.

Her bottom lip quivered. "But I never before thought marriage was a possibility. I have to think. I don't want to make a mistake that will hurt a lot of people. I couldn't live with myself if I did." She pressed her hand to his cheek. "Do you understand?"

He wanted to hug her. He wanted to fall on his knees and ask her to marry him. But at the strain around her eyes he pushed aside his own desires and pulled her close, brushing each damp eyelid with his fingertips and stroking her glassy-smooth hair.

When she sighed and relaxed in his arms, the tension slipped from his spine where it had dug in long bony fingers.

The door slammed shut in the next yard, reminding them of what lay outside the shelter of each other's arms.

Sighing gently, Laureen pulled back. "I need to go home. I promised Marj she'd get away early tonight."

She paused for a moment, still in the circle of his arms. He sensed her wonder and worry.

"We'll talk later," he promised.

She nodded and moved away, pausing at the door. "I almost forgot my excuse for coming. When do you want Kyler to come over again?"

"Tomorrow works for me. Will you bring him?"

Her eyes sparkling, she said, "Yes."

"Until tomorrow, then."

"Until tomorrow," she echoed then hurried away.

He stared after her for a long time. Long after she'd shut the gate behind her. He stood there even after he heard the door in the next yard close and knew she had gone inside.

She'd admitted she thought of him and marriage and family in the same context.

But she was holding back. She knew she would have to choose to put marriage and family ahead of her work at the home.

Would she? Could she?

There was only one way to find out. Ask her.

It scared him to think of the possibility she might not choose what he wanted. But remembering her response in this very room, he clung to the hope she would give the answer he ached for.

He'd talk to her the first chance he had.

He grabbed his jacket and headed for his truck. A few minutes later he stopped outside Freetown Nursing Home. Inside he made his way to his uncle Norman's room.

"Hi, Pete," the older man greeted him.

Pete recognized one of his uncle's clearer days. And he was right. Uncle Norman wanted to talk about his children. Always such conversations revolved around Pete's cousins, Carol and Bob. Uncle Norman never mentioned Billy, the boy who was responsible for the breakup of the family.

Pete sat quietly at his uncle's side, letting him talk about events that occurred years ago, children he never saw anymore—a life that was over.

He came away from the visit more solidly convinced he was right in believing few of these kids benefited from being placed with families.

He corrected himself. The children perhaps did benefit. But the families suffered untold harm.

He had utmost respect for the work Laureen did, but he failed to share her idealistic hopes for the future.

nine

Pete had hoped to talk to Laureen the next day when she brought Kyler over, but the boy needed more attention than usual as he filed the arm on his wooden figure.

At first Kyler refused to speak, but with a little encouragement Pete soon had him talking.

"He doesn't talk at the home anymore," Laureen whispered.

"Can't say I blame him." Pete had seen Michael's anger. "Don't we all find it safer to avoid contact with angry people?"

She nodded. "I guess so. But it's a little disappointing. He won't even talk to Marj."

They stood a few feet away from where Kyler bent over his woodwork, his tongue protruding out one corner of his mouth as he gently smoothed away a rough spot on the wooden arm.

Pete had never seen anyone with such infinite patience in bringing what he wanted out of a piece of wood.

"I think he likes being here," he said to Laureen. "The tension seems to slip from his shoulders when he begins to work."

Laureen slanted a look at him. "Pete, I sometimes think you're half blind. It isn't the work that makes him relax. It's feeling safe. And it's you, you big lug, who makes him feel safe."

Her gaze held him like a pair of silken arms. It made him warm inside to think a troubled little kid like Kyler felt safe with him. He looked deep into Laureen's eyes. Did she feel safe with him, too? What a weird thing to think. Why would she need to feel safe?

Maybe, he reasoned, safe wasn't the right word. Yet perhaps in an emotional sense that's what they both looked for. He wanted to know it was safe to love her. And Laureen? What emotional safety did she want? He wasn't sure. He wished he could talk to her, but she told Kyler it was time to go home.

"I wish we could stay longer, but I have to supervise the boys cleaning their rooms." She paused at the doorway, Kyler's hand in hers. "I miss our leisurely visits."

"Me, too."

Every evening it was the same—some intense time with Kyler, a few scattered moments with Laureen, but no time to talk or hold her. By Friday his thoughts had grown knotted and tangled as he thought of different ways of presenting his questions, dismissing each approach out of hand, then reconsidering it. He didn't know how much longer he could stand the suspense.

He would have put Kyler's lesson off until Monday except the boy had almost finished the man figure and practically begged to be allowed to complete it before the weekend. Something about the boy's eager request Pete couldn't refuse. Especially when he grabbed Pete's hand and looked at him so expectantly. Pete had never considered himself a softy, but Kyler had a way of making it a delight to do things for him. Pete smiled as he realized the kid had earned both his respect and admiration. He thought the little guy was neat.

Which meant he'd have to go another day or more without a chance to talk to Laureen.

He bent his attention back to Kyler, guiding his hand as he smoothed the bottom of the man figure. Laureen hovered at his shoulder. He knew he would never forget the scent of her as long as he lived. He'd always associate it with this warm and cozy feeling of the three of them working together and remember this tenuous feeling of waiting for their relationship to blossom.

He wouldn't let himself use the "love" word. Not yet. Not until he knew there was a chance for them to work out a permanent commitment, but in his mind the smell of a clean, fresh breeze with just a hint of wild flowers would make him think of Laureen at his side.

"Is it done?" Kyler asked, rubbing his thumb across the bottom.

"See if it will stand firm."

Kyler set the wooden figure on the table top, laughing quietly when the figure stood straight and true.

"Looks like your man is all finished," Pete said, patting the boy on the head. "You did a fine job, too. Don't you think so?"

Kyler nodded, turning his bright-eyed gaze to Pete. "It's perfect."

Pete nodded. For a kid not yet six, the work was exceptional.

"Can I take him home just for tomorrow?"

Pete glanced at Laureen. She shrugged. He turned back to Kyler. "It's yours. You can do what you want with it, but if you want to enter it in the fair it should look like new."

He nodded. "I'll be careful. It's just for tomorrow."

Pete couldn't help being curious. "Did you have something special in mind?"

Kyler ducked his head. "I want to show it to them." The boy's quiet words were almost too soft to hear.

"Them?" He looked at Laureen for an explanation. She wore a stunned look.

"Do you mean your new mom and dad, Kyler?"

He gave them a fleeting nod, his admiring gaze on the man figure in his hands.

"Well, now that is a special reason," Pete said. "You take your man home and take good care of it. Your new mom and dad will be real surprised at the talented little boy they're getting." Kyler gave him a pleased look and headed toward home. Pete watched him go, a tremble of worry bothering him. Would the young couple realize how special this crude carving was? To the inexperienced eye it lacked grace, but for someone who knew how difficult carving was, it was a work of sheer genius.

"They'd better appreciate it," he mumbled under his breath.

"What's that?" Laureen asked.

He shook off his concern. "I was just hoping the new mom and dad would see what skill it is for his age."

She nodded, watching Kyler enter the gate of the next yard and go inside. "I do, too."

When she started to follow Kyler home, Pete knew he had to grab his chance. "Do you have to hurry away?"

"I guess not."

"Then why don't we celebrate?"

An impish twinkle flashed across her eyes. "Don't tell me it's your birthday and no one has even mentioned it?"

"Nope, not my birthday, and I'm grateful. They seem to come a lot faster than they used to."

"Isn't that a fact?" She eyed him. "But you're young yet." She bent closer and peered at his head. "No gray hair, but then only the hairdresser knows for sure, right?"

He nodded. "You've never said how old you are."

"Guess."

"Okay." He pretended to study her hair, but in truth he had closed his eyes so he could breath in the scent of her and dream his dreams. Pulling himself back abruptly before he got carried away and made a fool of himself, he stepped away, crossed his arms over his chest, and tilted his head as he gave her a slow assessment. "But you have to promise you won't hit me if I miss it by a mile."

With a sniff of disdain she pulled herself tall. "I don't hit. Except in emergencies."

"I'll bet you'd consider it an emergency if I guessed forty years old." He laughed and ducked away at the shocked look on her face. "Sorry. I couldn't resist trying to get a rise out of you."

"Oh, you." She straightened up. "Go ahead. Guess."

He shook his head again. "I don't think so."

"You're chicken." She stuck her hands under her arms and strutted back and forth. "Cluck, cluck, cluck."

"Better a live chicken than a dead fool."

"Cluck, cluck, cluck."

"How does chicken soup sound to you?"

"Clucccccck." She ended on a strangled note. "Okay. I'll make it easy for you. How good are you at simple math?"

"Can I use a calculator?"

"Only if you don't mind being called a cheat."

He laughed. "Cheat. Chicken. You think I should mind?"

She waved her hand. "Can't see why. But I'll be easy on you."

He looked toward the ceiling. "Why is it I don't believe that?"

"Now pay attention."

"Yes, teacher." He sounded as painfully resigned as he could, but he didn't mind her teasing one bit. He found this side of her delightfully refreshing.

"You ready?"

"I'm as ready as I'm ever going to be."

"Here goes. I spent five years at home, twelve years in school, thirteen counting kindergarten, spent two summers volunteering at a small mission in Mexico. I went to university for four years, worked part of a year as a nanny for a handicapped child, spent the rest of that year as a nanny for three children in the Bahamas then went back for my master's. Worked a year at a crisis center, and I've been with the Barnabas Association for three, almost four, years."

He had all his fingers used up long before she'd finished, and he stared at her in defeat. "Come on, Laureen. You don't really expect me to keep track of all that?"

"It's just a few simple numbers. How hard can it be?"

"Let's start at the beginning—"

"I was born a tiny baby—"

"Not that beginning. I'll assume you were eighteen when you graduated from high school. And then you did some summer stuff then went to university. I got that far. That makes you about twenty-two. Then what?"

In a slow, syllable-by-syllable explanation, she said, "Summers at a mission in Mexico—"

"Summers don't really count, do they?"

She shrugged. "That's up to you. Then nanny for a handicapped little boy, nanny for three rambunctious kids in the Bahamas—"

"That must have been a real hardship—the beach and sun and ocean and all."

"You have no idea." She wiped her brow. "A veritable sentence in the salt mines."

"Yeah, right, but could you be a little more specific as to how much time passed?"

She fluttered her hands. "Seemed like an eternity at the time."

He made a choking motion with his hands. "Laureen. . . ."

"Oh, all right, if you want to be that way. It was less than a year."

"Okay, so that puts you at twenty-three?"

"I don't know. Aren't you doing the math?"

"I'm trying. Then back to university?"

"Yup. Did my master's."

"In two years?"

"But don't forget the time I spent back at the mission in Mexico."

"How could I? That would have been a year? Or the summer?"

"Yup. It would have been."

"You're just trying to confuse me, aren't you?"

"Me? I wouldn't think of it."

"So the summer in Mexico?"

"Two summers."

He flicked his hands. "So that doesn't really count, either. And then you began work here?"

"Don't forget the crisis center."

He pressed his palm to his forehead. "Right. Is there anything you haven't done?"

She laughed. "There must be something, somewhere."

He groaned. "How long were you at the crisis center?"

" 'Til I got sick of it."

"Okay, so three days doesn't really count so we can forget that little sojourn."

She laughed outright. "Almost a year."

He ticked off another finger. "So now you're twenty-four." He knew better than to frame it as a question. "And three, almost four years here. So"—he held up three fingers, hesitating at the fourth—"you're twenty-eight, maybe twenty-nine years old."

"I am?" She looked as if he'd announced that her name had changed. "When did I get to be so old?" She patted her hair and twisted her head back and forth checking out as much of herself as she could see. "Oh, well, seems I still have all my parts, and as far as I know they still work."

He laughed.

She gave him a pleased look. "So are we celebrating your birthday?"

It took him a moment to catch up with her twist of conversation; then he recalled he'd suggested she should spend some time with him celebrating. "No birthday, but we should celebrate Kyler finishing his first figure."

"And wanting to show it to his new mom and dad."

"For sure."

"I'll run over and let Marj know I'll be away." And she disappeared before he could say anything more.

He paced the yard as he waited for her to return, rehearsing what he would say to her. Everything he came up with sounded strained. He still hadn't found the right way when she breezed through the back gate, wearing a sky-blue dress that swung when she walked.

He crossed his arms and watched her.

She grinned and marched right up to him. "I'm here. Where's the party?"

He grinned down at her. "Who said anything about a party?"

She widened her eyes and looked confused. "Celebrate. Party?" She stepped back. "You mean there's no party?" And fixing him with a stern look she planted her hands on her hips. "Mister, you got me here under false pretenses."

"Would you settle for dinner and a drive?"

She tipped her head back and forth. "No party?"

He shook his head.

"Okay." Before he could react, she hooked her arm inside his elbow and pulled him toward the gate. "Let's go."

He laughed all the way to the truck where he helped her step up. With no plan in mind he headed for the highway. The idea of driving along the pavement, covering the miles with her teasing and laughing at his side, pulled him like a magnet. "Where should we go?" he asked as he pulled up to the stop sign.

Waving her arm in an all-encompassing gesture, she gave a large sigh. "The world beckons."

"I don't think I have enough gas to make it around the world. Would you settle for a drive in the country?"

"Yep. I'm getting used to settling for second best around here. First no party, and now no world trip."

He remembered a small country restaurant with lots of atmosphere and good food. And a suitable distance away. He turned west, reveling in the straight road, the open spaces, and the woman at his side. He couldn't remember when he'd felt so satisfied with life. Only one thing would make it better— Laureen's agreeing they would be a forever couple. And to-night he intended to find out if that was possible.

"Where are we going?" she demanded.

"Can you stand to let it be a surprise?"

"Of course." She wiggled back in the seat as if to prove she wasn't even curious. "You think I'm a kid who can't wait?"

"Is that what you think?"

"That's what I think you think."

"You think so, do you?" He smiled at her.

He turned onto a secondary road and slowed down for a tractor and cultivator crossing the road. They passed pretty farms with red barns, full shelterbelts of trees, and yards with groomed lawns and abundant flowers.

Laureen inched forward. "It's beautiful out here."

"It is." He turned again, to the west, and soon they were in rolling country, the ravines dark with pines. The view of the mountains from the high places was spectacular.

"Do you mind stopping?" she said as they crested another hill.

A little alarmed at the urgency in her voice, he braked and pulled to the shoulder. He had barely stopped when she jumped from the truck.

He hurried to her side wondering if she felt sick to her stomach, but she leaned against the truck and lifted her face to the breeze.

"Isn't this a gorgeous view?"

He shifted his gaze toward the sweeping vista. "It's fantastic." The hill fell away steeply to a deep narrow valley. And then climbed again, in ever-rising folds to the rock-faced mountains. But it wasn't the mountains that drew his interest. It was Laureen, and he turned back to watch her.

Her eyes shone blue, deeper in color than the sky. He didn't know much about jewels or gems, but he guessed no semiprecious stone came close to the pure, shining beauty of her eyes. Her hair reflected the brightness of the sun. If he could catch that dark sheen in a bottle and sell it for furniture finish, he'd be a millionaire, he thought, amused by the direction of his thoughts.

She lifted her arms above her head and laughed. "How can anyone look at a scene like this and not believe in God? It's beauty beyond imagination."

He looked again at the scene before them. "It's amazing how much beauty God has put in the world." He wanted to catch the woman at his side, but before he gave himself permission to truly love her he had to know what she intended for their relationship.

"I'm getting awfully hungry," he complained.

"Not one to be satisfied with the offerings of nature?"

He loved the teasing note in her voice. It sent waves of enjoyment through him. He could hardly wait to find out if he had a chance with her.

They returned to the truck and continued their journey, then arrived at the hideaway he had in mind. Only two other vehicles were parked outside the large weathered log building that had once served as a hunting lodge. Hunters still came, but so did people from every walk of life. They came for the homemade food, and they came for the surroundings.

Pete parked and hurried to open the door for Laureen.

"What is this place?" she asked. "Are you sure they serve meals?"

"I'm sure. Why? Have you decided drinking in the beauties of nature doesn't satisfy stomach hunger?"

Her stomach growled, and she laughed. "Does that answer your question?"

"By the sounds of it we'd better hurry." He took her hand and raced toward the lodge.

Inside the door an older couple, owners and operators,

greeted them. The gentleman took one look at their clasped hands and led them to a quiet table next to a window overlooking the river valley. He listed the specialties of the day and waited while they discussed their choices, then hurried away. A few minutes later he reappeared with large steaming cups of coffee then slipped away so quickly Pete didn't even get a chance to voice his thank-you.

The roast beef and baked potatoes were perfect. The vegetables crisp and hot. The homemade apple pie the best he'd ever tasted, but it all paled in comparison to the pleasure of having Laureen across the table from him, laughing and teasing.

He waited until the dishes had been removed and fresh coffee filled their cups before he leaned toward her, taking both her hands in his.

"Laureen, I really enjoy your company. I don't know when I've had more fun."

She wrinkled her nose. "How quickly you forget how often I run to cry on your shoulder."

He shrugged. "Can't say I haven't enjoyed parts of that, too."

She snorted. "Let me guess. The part where I moaned about my worries, right?"

He squeezed her hands and grew serious.

She sobered instantly.

He looked deep into her eyes and found depths that encouraged him to hope she might want the same things he did.

"Laureen, I think I'm falling in love with you. Tell me—do I have a chance?"

ten

Laureen let her hands rest in Pete's grasp even though she had a strong urge to hug her arms around herself and laugh. He'd said the words she'd longed to hear. Or, at least, almost said them. He wanted to know if he had a chance. If only he knew. *Careful, Laureen.* She took a deep breath and whispered a silent prayer for wisdom.

"I've been thinking of you a lot lately," she said.

He squeezed her hands. "In a good way, I hope."

She nodded, her eyes feeling too bright. "In a very good way."

"And?"

"Remember my vow? To never hurt one of these children by putting my own needs above theirs?"

The joy fled from his eyes. He loosened his grip on her hands, but she squeezed so he couldn't pull away.

"I asked God to show me what was right for me," she hurried on, desperate to remove the anxious tension from around his eyes. "I told Him if this was His will He'd have to work things out so I wouldn't break my vow."

She could tell by his puzzled look he hadn't made the connection. "And then Kyler begins to talk, and it looks as if he'll be going to a permanent home soon. And then, out of the blue, Michael and Davey's mother shows up wanting them back." She lifted one shoulder. "It looks as if they'll all be gone by the end of the summer."

He seemed stunned.

"So you see—I'm free to do what I want without hurting one of the children."

"Are you saying as long as the boys are safely taken care of you and I have a chance?"

She moved her head up and down slightly. She'd expected a little more enthusiasm from him. After all he was the one who'd brought up the subject. "A very good chance," she added, in case he still didn't get it.

He leaned closer, his eyes dark, steady.

She held very still, mesmerized by the power of his gaze. "Is that what you want?" she asked.

He nodded once. "Yes."

"Yes? That's it?"

"No, you silly woman. That isn't all. I love you. You're the sun and moon and stars of my world." He jumped up, pulling her to her feet. "Come on—let's get out of here so we can talk." He paused to pay the bill, then practically dragged her toward the truck. Halfway across the parking lot he switched directions and headed for a path leading into the darkening woods.

"Where are we going?"

"For a walk."

"Look here, mister. You say you love me, and then you want to go for a walk. If you don't kiss me real soon, I'm going to explode. And that would not be a pretty sight."

He ducked down the path. "Ah, privacy." Without further ado he pulled her into his arms. But he didn't kiss her right away. "I love you, Laureen. I want to marry you."

She wrapped her arms around his waist. "Pete, you big lug, I love you so much I can hardly stand it. Yes, I'll marry you. Yes, yes, yes. A thousand times, yes."

His lips muffled the last few words.

Darkness had fallen before they finished their walk, but it seemed they had so many things to talk about.

Pete helped her into the truck kissing her nose before he shut the door.

He climbed behind the wheel but didn't immediately start the motor. "How long do we have to wait until we get married?"

He teased a lock of hair behind her ear, making it difficult for her to think, but they needed to discuss some things. "How do you feel about my working?"

"I kind of thought you would want to. I don't mind so long as you're home in the evenings when I'm home."

"I'll be yours always and forever. I thought I could continue working in the home but as day staff, not live-in."

He tightened his arms around her. "I wouldn't want you being live-in anywhere but with me."

She giggled at his gruff voice. "Sounds good to me. It will take a little while to find a replacement at the home, but it's the best time of year to do it—just before staff returns. Gone before school starts and a new batch of boys arrive." She turned so she could watch the look on Pete's face as she finally gave the answer to his question. "How would you feel about a September wedding?"

Disbelief raced across his face and then a look of adoration that made her realize even more how special this man was. "I was afraid you'd want to wait a year or two." His laugh rang with joy. "Yes, September is just fine."

"That only gives us six or seven weeks to plan a wedding."

"Can you do that?"

"If we don't have a great big splash." She told him of her dream wedding—just family, a quiet dinner afterward. "I couldn't stand all that hoopla."

"Sounds good to me." He kissed her.

She sighed. She would cherish his love as long as she lived.

❧

Two days later, when the administration announced there would be a meeting regarding Michael and Davey, Laureen was prepared. She knew the decision had been made to allow their mother to regain custody. She'd seen it coming and even welcomed it in a way, knowing she was powerless to stop it. She saw it as part of God's plan for opening up the way for her to marry Pete.

An off-site visit was arranged for the two boys the following Saturday. Kyler had another visit with his new mom and dad. Details had been worked out with the goal of having him in his new home by the beginning of September.

Laureen informed her bosses of her desire to turn the supervisor's role over to someone else. She would begin her part of the interview process as soon as the application deadline passed. She'd been given assurances that a temporary supervisor would be in place in time for her wedding if a permanent one hadn't been found by then.

She and Pete had decided to get married in a quiet ceremony at the church she'd attended growing up and to ask her parents if they could hold the reception at the old family house. Laureen planned to hire a caterer to serve a hot meal to the family members who would be her only guests.

With the boys all gone on visits, her Saturday was free. She and Pete planned to drive the fifty miles to the small town she'd grown up in and visit her parents.

She couldn't believe how much she looked forward to a whole day to enjoy Pete's company.

Although they could have arrived at her parents' in a little over an hour, Laureen had other plans. She knew Pete enjoyed discovering local history. His stories had given her a new appreciation for Freetown.

Today would be her turn.

They drove out of town and headed east. Within a few minutes the land grew almost level. They were entering the prairie area of Alberta.

"Slow down," she told him after they'd driven for three quarters of an hour. "I want you to make a turn up ahead."

In answer to the questioning look he gave her, she said, "The folks aren't expecting us until later this afternoon."

He squeezed her hand. "Sounds good to me."

"I have some special stuff I want to show you. Turn here."

They turned onto a gravel road. After a few miles she pointed out a trail. "We take that now."

He turned but pulled to a halt. "You've got to be kidding. It's nothing more than a cow path."

"Wrong. It's actually an old wagon trail. People used to haul hay from the river valley to their farms. It's perfectly safe, believe me." She didn't tell him it had been ten years or more since she'd been this way. She hoped she could remember the directions clearly.

He put the truck in gear and inched forward, muttering about prairie trails as they bounced over the rough ground. A mile or so later she recognized the place and ordered Pete to pull over.

"From here we walk," she told him, jumping down from the truck while he sat staring at her. "Come on. You won't be sorry."

She parted the barbed wires on the fence and slipped through, careful not to catch her shirt on the barbs. He pushed the upper wire down and swung his leg over. Dust rose from every step they took. The scent of sage and grass and wild roses carried on the breeze.

"Is it always this windy?" he asked, as a gust swept up the gully.

"This is nothing. If you're not from the prairie you don't know wind."

She ran ahead of him, laughing as the wind tore at her breath. She spun around to face him. "I love the spaces. On a clear day you can see forever." She studied the distant gray-green horizon.

"Are we in Saskatchewan?" His voice registered suspicion.

"Miles from it. Have you never been out this way?"

"I've driven through it a time or two."

"With your pedal to the metal, I'll bet." She shook her head sadly. "The only way to enjoy the prairie is to slow down and see it."

"What's to see?" he growled.

"Grass and sky. Birds and flowers. And lots more. Hurry up." She bent forward, climbing to the top of the deceptively gentle hill.

Pete followed. The wind caught him as he reached the peak, and he ducked. "Man, that barbed wire sure doesn't stop much wind."

She laughed as he came to her side. "There it is." She pointed.

He looked around. "I don't see anything."

"The rocks. See how they form the shape of a man." She ran to the right. "This is his head." She hurried around. "Here is one arm pointing upward, above his head. And here're his legs, though one leg has been missing a foot as long as anyone can remember. And here's his other foot. And his other arm. See—he's holding a spear or something." She returned to his side.

"What is it?"

"A stone effigy. No one knows a lot about it, but the experts think a great Indian chief died here while on a hunting trip. The warriors left this to show how important a man he was. Maybe it was because they couldn't get him back to the sacred burial ground or something."

"He must have been a big man."

"I guess so."

"This thing must be over thirty feet long. He must have been *real* big."

Laughing, she slipped her arm through his. "He was nothing. I know someone who is far more important than he, no matter how big he was." The wind whipped her hair across her cheeks as she lifted her face to him. He smiled down at her, tucking the strands of hair behind her ears.

"Sounds like someone I should be careful of. Your father, maybe?"

"Him you should probably be careful of, but you know I was talking about you. You"—she reached her hands around his neck and pulled his head closer—"you are the most important thing in the world to me."

"Good." And finally he kissed her. A flood of love poured through her with such force her knees grew weak. She wouldn't have stayed on her feet if Pete's arms hadn't been holding her so tightly. Never in her whole life, in her whole world to date, had her universe shrunk to one pair of arms and one set of lips and two hearts beating as one. Yet, at the same time, it seemed as if the horizons had bolted far away, opening up spaces in her mind and heart.

She stepped away. "We're not finished. One more thing you have to see while we're here." She rushed them down a gentle slope and up another until they crested the tallest of the undulating hills. "It's a medicine wheel," she said, pointing to the vast circle of rocks, intersected into pie-shaped, rock-bound segments. The point of each segment met in the center marked by a huge pile of rocks. Odd rocks lay scattered in some of the pie segments.

"Tell me about it."

"There isn't a lot to tell. No one is sure what it's for. Anthropologists have studied it. Native people have visited. They are certain it's part of a sacred ceremony, but no one has given a clear explanation." She led him to the far side where a path led to the center. "Some think it has something to do with a sun ceremony. Others say perhaps it was part of some mystical search for successful hunting.

"Huh. Very interesting." Pete retraced his steps out of the circle and walked around the outer perimeter. He faced her, his arms crossed over his chest. "Here's my theory. It's a map."

She hooted. "You've got to be kidding. How do you fold it to put it in the glove box? Or a saddlebag?"

"Yes, I'm sure it's a map. See these scattered rocks?" He pointed out several in the wedge shapes. "Bet no one had any reason for them. Bet they said someone had desecrated the site?" When she nodded, he said, "Thought so. My theory makes a lot more sense. See that big rock points north, right?"

Laureen agreed.

"And all these shapes point to the center. See—we're at the central spot. Say we were one hunting party. We decide to go over there because we saw some elephants or something good to eat."

Laureen shook her head. "This is Alberta, not Africa."

He waved a dismissive hand. "Don't ruin my story."

"Sorry." She flashed her palms toward him. "But are you sure the wind hasn't loosened a few of your shingles?"

"My shingles are firmly in place though I'm about to lose my shirt in this hurricane."

She giggled at the way his soft green, button-front shirt billowed around him like a sail. "You look like you're about to take flight."

He shoved the bottom of his shirt firmly into the waist of his pants before he turned back to his explanation. "Now pay attention and stop trying to distract me."

She sketched a salute. "Yes, sir—sir."

"So one party has gone over there to hunt—"

"Elephants, wasn't it?"

He ignored her except for the look he flashed her. "So how do they let the other hunting parties know where they are? Easy, I say."

"Um hum."

"The elephant party"—he slanted a teasing look at her—"is also the gray party. So they put their gray rock here." He stepped to the wedge indicating the direction he had chosen. "Now when the next party returns they know they've gone over there. And they decide to go that way." He pointed another direction. "They're the green party so they put their greenish rock in this section." He put a pebble in the correct place. "See. It's a map."

Her mouth hung open. "That is really clever." She was impressed.

He stepped closer and smiled at her. She knew her whole life had been moving toward this moment. She knew she was meant to be with this man for the rest of her life. She knew she had been created to be his, and he had been created to be hers.

She clung to his hand as they made their way back to the truck.

"What's next, sweet Laureen?" he asked as they sat in the cab.

"I'll take you to a favorite place of mine when I was a child."

She directed him back to the highway and a few miles down the road had him turn north. Again they had to leave the good roads and use a dusty trail, this one sandy and wide.

"We are going to something or someplace, aren't we?" Pete demanded after they'd been on the trail fifteen minutes.

"We're almost there." At that moment a puddle of water appeared on their left. The trail followed the water's shape until suddenly a larger body of water appeared. "This is it. An old Canadian National Railway dam. It hasn't been used by the CNR since they switched to diesel engines." She directed him to pull over when they were close to the dam itself.

She scrunched up her forehead. "It's not quite how I remember it."

"When were you last here?"

"It must be fifteen years ago. Where does the time go?" She glanced around. "There used to be picnic tables and outhouses and campers and—" She broke off. "We used to come on the weekend and fish. We'd camp overnight and build a big fire and roast marshmallows and get up early and fry bacon over the campfire and fish some more, then rush home to shower and go to church. It was so much fun."

Pete grinned at her. "You're pulling my leg. You used to fish in this dam?"

"I'll have you know the water is sixty-some feet deep. The

government used to stock it. Every year they'd bring out barrels of fingerlings and dump them in the water."

The skeptical look never left his face.

"Come on. I'll show you." She led him to the earthen bank holding the water back and took him to the middle so he could see how far below them the ground lay. "Are you convinced?"

"Maybe."

"There might even be fish left here. There were always stories about those big suckers who survived winter after winter. We could see them jumping." She turned toward the water, but except for the skiff of ripples from the wind the surface remained flat.

"Come on. I'll show you one of our favorite parts of coming to the dam." She led him across the earth embankment to the cement spillway. They pushed through the iron-barred gate. "There were all sorts of traditions about climbing up the spillway. The first time everyone tried to scare you to death. After you'd been through a few times, the challenge was to find new ways to get that fright."

"Great," he muttered. "Sounds like an initiation rite. And let me guess—I'm about to be initiated?"

She arched one eyebrow at him. "Afraid?"

He studied her face. "Should I be?"

She rounded her eyes and looked innocent. "A big boy like you? I wouldn't think so." She headed into the cement tunnel. "Come on—I'll even lead the way."

He was right on her heels. "Why do I get the feeling I'm going to regret this?"

She followed the tunnel around a corner and was engulfed in darkness so complete it took her breath away just as it had when she was a child. A cool breeze tickled around her ankles.

"Watch your head. It gets lower as we go along. Put your hands on the walls to feel your way." She had planned to hurry ahead silently, as her brothers had done when she was a kid. They had left her gasping for breath in the darkness. She wanted to see if she could scare Pete as much as they had scared her, but she stumbled on a rock and gasped. In the darkness she felt disoriented and confused.

"Laureen, are you okay?" The rumble of his deep voice calmed her.

"Yes. Watch for rocks."

She took a deep breath and edged forward. *Quiet,* she silently ordered herself. *Don't make a sound.* Holding her breath she pressed to one side of the narrowing tunnel and kept very still. A tickle of laughter started in her stomach but didn't get any further as the silence deepened. She strained for some sound. Nothing. Where was Pete?

Darkness and silence pressed in on her. She imagined she could hear water dripping someplace, and the thought of being in the tunnel if it began to fill with water choked her so she couldn't breath. She clenched her fists and pressed them to her thighs. *I am too old to panic the way I did when I was eight. If I just take a deep breath I'll be okay.* But the air was too heavy to breath.

Where, oh, where was Pete? Why didn't he make a sound so she'd know where he was? Why didn't he call out with a thread of fear in his voice so she could call off this stupid game? She clenched her teeth so hard a pain sliced through the back of her head.

I'll count to ten before I panic. One, two, three, four— Something warm brushed her arm. A scream escaped her tight throat, echoing up and down the tunnel like a haunting moan.

eleven

The touch on her arm steadied. In the back of her brain she realized it was too warm to be a snake. Not furry enough to be a small animal. It registered with maddening slowness that it had a familiar feel. She stopped screaming.

"You think you're so funny, don't you?" It was hard to sound convincingly annoyed with a quiver in her voice.

His deep rolling chuckle bounced against the walls. "You're mad because I caught you in your own trap."

Unashamedly she found his hand. "You almost scared me to death. Then what would you have done? How would you explain my body in this tunnel? Huh. Did you think of that?" She inched along the tunnel as she talked, clinging to the warmth of his hand even though it made it difficult to find her way. She scraped her knuckles along the wall.

"We have to be almost out of here." She'd forgotten how long the complete darkness lasted.

"Look ahead. There's a square of light showing."

"Good." She kept her eyes on the light, relief sluicing through her when the walls grew visible.

Finally they were out. She swept her hands over her hair and clothing to make sure no spiders or bugs had hitched a free ride. Shivers snaked up and down her arms. "Ooh. I hate that place."

Pete leaned against the cement frame, his arms cradled over his chest, a teasing smile on his lips. "So why did you take me there?"

She darted him an exasperated look. "You were the one who was supposed to be scared. Not me." She straightened and fixed him with her most annoyed expression. "I should have left you in there."

He laughed. "Oh, yes, Miss Tough Guy. I bet you couldn't go through the tunnel by yourself. You'd turn into a basket case, and someone would have to rescue you."

Just the thought of it made her shudder, and she grimaced.

"Serves you right for trying to trick me." He lifted one arm and pulled her to him. "Let this be a lesson to you in the future." But she didn't care what he said so long as he held her against his chest where she could hear the reassuring beat of his heart against her cheek.

It was late afternoon before they headed down the street to the house where Laureen had grown up and where her parents still lived.

"I better warn you to expect a complete inquisition. I'm still their little girl. I don't think they thought I'd ever get married so they've taken on the role of protectors and supporters. They'll want to know everything about you."

"I have nothing to hide."

"You'll have no secrets either when they get through with you."

He squeezed his arm across her shoulders. "I'm glad they take good care of you. Don't worry. I think I can give them all the reassurance they need."

⁂

Pete pulled her close, loving the feel of her against his side. He breathed in the scent of her perfume and let the sweetness of her fill him. She had proven to be a delight beyond his greatest expectations. Funny, teasing, amusing, and so totally giving in her affections. There seemed to be a readiness to reveal her love. He was so glad she wanted to get married right away. He wanted her with him always and forever.

Of course, her parents might be a little concerned at their haste, which was only natural. He would do his best to put their worries at ease.

He stopped in front of the house Laureen pointed out. He didn't have the engine shut off before a man and a woman hurried down the sidewalk. Laureen's parents. Her father was tall and dark-haired like Laureen. Her mother looked too young to be Laureen's mother. He didn't have time to think of anything else before Laureen dragged him from the truck and led him to meet her parents.

"Nice to meet the man who has convinced Laureen there is something in life besides her work," Mr. Baker said. He rubbed Laureen's shoulder. "It's obvious she's fallen head over heels in love. Look at the way she glows."

"Supper's ready," Mrs. Baker said, after kissing Pete's cheek. "Let's go inside."

Over the meal, as if by unspoken agreement, the conversation consisted of catching up on the events of all the family members. Laureen's parents studied him unobtrusively. Several times he caught them exchanging glances and knew he was being measured and weighed.

The inquisition, as Laureen called it, was only being delayed until the meal was over.

They had thick pieces of moist chocolate cake topped with ice cream for dessert and then another round of coffee. Pete settled back and enjoyed the conversation. He wasn't nervous about the questions they'd ask. He figured once they saw he loved Laureen and how he longed to spend the rest of his life making her happy, they would accept him wholeheartedly.

Laureen and her mother cleared up the meal things.

"We'll do the dishes later," Mrs. Baker announced. "Let's go sit in the living room where it's more comfortable."

This was it.

Pete smiled across at Laureen.

She tilted her head slightly, a teasing grin on her lips.

"Tell us about your family," Mr. Baker began.

Pete gave a brief description of his brother and sister and parents.

"Will they have any problem getting here for the wedding?"

"I've talked to them all, and they promise they'll make it."

"How long have you been a Christian?" Laureen's mother asked.

He told them about the church he'd grown up in, the influence of his parents and grandparents, and his early struggles with choosing his way or God's way. "I guess I was afraid if I put Him first, He'd ask me to go to Africa and preach to the cannibals. I couldn't get past the thought of a boiling pot of oil with Pete Long the specialty of the day."

Everyone chuckled. "I know it was stupid," he continued. "But I was a kid. Now I know it's okay for me to fix pipes, too. And love Laureen and plan on spending the rest of my life with her."

Laureen's parents smiled across the room at each other. "That's all we want for our daughter," Mr. Baker said. "Someone who will cherish her as much as we do."

He knew they'd accepted him.

❧

Laureen sang as she completed the reports for the weekend. Davey and Michael seemed resigned, even accepting, of the plan for them to join their mother and new stepfather.

Kyler had come back smiling and happy. *And Laureen,* she felt like writing, *had a marvelous time on the weekend.* Her parents liked Pete from the outset. They'd been impressed with his quiet steadiness.

"He's a good balance for you," her dad said, as if she were wild and uncontrolled. But she agreed. She and Pete were a perfect balance. It didn't matter if she were serious, teasing, or even downright silly, he was the same, steady Pete, always responding in just the right way to make her feel cherished and appreciated.

He'd taken her to visit his uncle Norman in the nursing home. The man appeared not to know they were there, and after a few minutes of reading the Bible to him they had slipped away.

"Some days he's better," Pete said. "But on his good days he pines for his family."

It was sad, Laureen agreed.

The doorbell sounded, but she let Marj answer it as she put the papers back in the file cabinet. When she heard voices in the living room she went out to investigate, surprised to see Kyler's adoptive parents. She shot Marj a questioning look, but Marj gave a slight shake of her head.

She couldn't imagine what had brought them to visit on a Monday afternoon, but the nervous look that passed between them sent a shiver up her spine.

"It's nice to see you," she began. "What can we do for you?"

The young man, Frank, could barely meet her gaze. "We need to talk to you. Something's come up."

Laureen knew it wasn't a something she was going to be glad to hear, but she held back any reaction until she had the facts.

Frank reached for his wife's hand. "We discovered just this morning that Ann is going to have a baby."

"Congratulations." A baby was good news for everyone, she hoped.

"We never thought we'd be able to have our own baby," Ann said. "The doctors said—well, it appears they were wrong."

"It won't make any difference to the adoption proceedings," she assured them. "A pregnancy is no longer a reason to stop an adoption."

Ann looked at Frank. He gave a small nod before he faced Laureen. "We never expected to have our own child. You see that's why we were so keen to adopt Kyler, but now—well, you see how it is."

Laureen clenched her hands together and took a deep breath. "I'm afraid I don't. How is it?" Oh, yes, she saw how it was all right; but she'd force them to say the words themselves.

"We can't go ahead with adoption."

"Can't or won't?" Not that she wanted Kyler to go where he would never be able to compete successfully with a new baby. But they talked as if they had no choice.

Ann leaned forward. "This is the most exciting thing that's ever happened to us. Surely you don't think we should take Kyler, too. We want to devote ourselves to our own child. It just wouldn't be fair not to."

"No, I suppose not." She took a deep breath, mentally pushing back the anger that blackened the edges of her mind. "Shall I call him in so you can tell him?"

Both faces before her grew panicked. "I'm sure you can do it much better than we can," Frank said, jerking to his feet. "Thank you for everything."

Marj showed them out then came back to the room. "Oh,

Laureen. This is awful. Poor little boy."

Laureen nodded. "And I have to find a way to break the news to him. Any suggestions?"

Marj shook her head. "You take some time to yourself to pray about it. I'll look after things."

Laureen went to her room. She sank into her chair and opened her Bible. But she didn't read. She felt like the bottom had fallen out of her world. Everything had worked out so well. All the boys going to permanent homes. Her wedding plans proceeding at a brisk rate. Now what? What did God want?

Of one thing she was certain—she couldn't think of leaving with Kyler heading into a crisis.

She still hadn't decided how to tell him the news when Pete arrived home and she realized she'd unconsciously been waiting to talk to him.

She rushed next door and threw herself into his arms, practically knocking him off his feet.

"Whoa, lady. Warn me before you tackle me." He kissed her gently and held her close for a minute before he asked, "What's wrong?"

"It's Kyler." As she explained, he led her inside and sat beside her on the couch, his arms around her.

"That's really tough," he said.

"I haven't told him yet. I don't know if I can."

"You don't have a choice."

"I know." Her insides twisted with misery. "And how can I think of leaving when he's going through this?"

His hug didn't relax; yet she felt his arms stiffen. Then he shook her slightly. "Laureen, you aren't leaving him. You'll be there every day. You'll be right next door where he can see you whenever he wants to."

"I guess so." Why had she thought it would be more of a separation? "I was too upset to think clearly."

"I can understand that. But we can go ahead with our wedding plans all the same."

She relaxed against him. "It's a good thing you can set things straight for me. Now if only I can find a way to tell Kyler."

"Why not bring him over to the shop where you can be alone with him?"

"That's ideal. It's a place that's special to him. Besides, I'll have your shoulder to cry on when I'm finished."

He hugged her close and kissed her.

She waited until after the boys had eaten supper before she took him over.

He took the wooden figure of the man with him. Upon arrival he hurried to the table where the other two pieces of wood were set out. Pete was there. "Do you want me to leave?" he asked Laureen.

"I'd prefer you stay." She knew Kyler had a special bond with Pete, and she hoped his presence would give him strength as much as it would her.

She pulled a chair close and drew him to her knees. "Kyler, honey, I have to tell you something."

The boy's glance darted to Pete and back to her. She and Pete had already told him about how they were going to get married. He had nodded his approval and said he was glad.

"It's not about Pete and me," she assured him. She wished it were. "It's about you and your new mom and dad." The words stuck in her throat. She wished she could have called Frank and Ann something besides mom and dad. Those titles should automatically mean security. "They're going to have a brand-new baby."

His eyes grew round. A frightened look crossed his face. Poor boy. He'd been around long enough to know good news for someone else often meant bad news for a kid from the home.

She wrapped her arms around him. "Kyler, they won't have time for a baby and a big boy." It was an outright lie, but how could she tell him the truth—that now they were having a child of their flesh and bones, adoption wasn't an option in their minds.

He pulled away and shuffled to the end of the table. "Kyler?"

He stared away from her.

Pete moved around to stand in front of the boy. "It's not because of you. You're a nice little boy that anyone would be proud to call a son."

Kyler stared at the floor.

Pete touched the thin shoulder. "Sometimes things just don't work out, and there's no one to blame."

The child nodded and slowly melted against Pete's legs, his small body quivering.

Pete squatted down and held the boy in his arms.

Kyler didn't cry. He seldom cried. But he shook like a blade of grass in a prairie wind.

Laureen swiped the back of her hand across her eyes as Pete held the boy, his head bent over Kyler's.

Kyler straightened. He looked at the pieces of wood on the table but made no move to pick them up.

"Do you want to do some carving?" Pete asked.

The boy shook his head.

"Would you like a soda?"

Again Kyler shook his head.

Laureen guessed Pete hoped to interest the boy in something that might distract him.

Kyler looked to Laureen and pointed toward home.

"You want to go?"

He nodded.

"Say good-bye to Pete."

He waved one small hand.

"You can take your man figure with you." Pete held it out to him, but Kyler shook his head. He took Laureen's hand and tugged her toward the door.

"I'll talk to you later," she promised Pete as she let Kyler pull her homeward.

~

It had been two weeks since Pete had watched Laureen break the awful news to Kyler. It wasn't fair to promise a child something that big and important and then change your mind. He began to understand Laureen's feelings about doing things to the kids in her care that would hurt them in such a profound way.

Two weeks, and Kyler had not said another word.

Pete was as concerned as Laureen.

She brought him over to work on his project. He obeyed his instructions, but his heart had gone out of his work.

Every night Pete and Laureen discussed their concerns for the boy. Pete stood with her in striving to provide as much support and security as she could for the boy.

"After we're married maybe you can bring him over often," he said.

"I will certainly want to give him as much attention as I can without being unfair to others in the home." At her troubled look he pulled her into his arms.

"I'd do anything I could to ease this for you." He kissed the top of her hair and rested his cheek there. If only he could take away the pain both Laureen and Kyler were feeling. But all he could do was encourage them and pray for them.

He smiled against the top of her head. "There's one good thing to come out of this."

"You're kidding, right?" Her voice was muffled against his chest. Her breath warmed a spot near his heart.

"I've never prayed so hard for one concern before in my life." He knew how much his words had meant to her when she slipped her arms around him and hugged him tight.

"It really helps to hear you say that." She sighed, and heat radiated like a sunburst around his heart. "If only he would talk."

"If only," he echoed. He'd enjoyed the times Kyler had told him what he saw in the wood and what he'd done in his day. Sure, the kid wasn't real talkative, but what he said carried a lot of weight. "Why don't the two of us take him out some-place special? Maybe that would help him realize there are still people who care for him."

Laureen agreed eagerly, and they planned an outing to the park.

Pete drove them to the park two days later. He knew there was no instant cure for Kyler's emotional problems, but he felt certain lots of time with people he felt safe with would help.

He'd brought a ball and headed for an open grassy spot. "Come on, Kyler. Let's play catch." He stepped back and tossed an easy throw to him.

Kyler lifted his hands and let the ball land in his grasp.

"Throw it to me," Laureen called.

With all the enthusiasm of a wilted plant Kyler tossed the ball.

"Okay," Laureen said, pounding the ball into her palm.

"Let's see how hard we can make Pete work."

She threw a hard one. Pete caught it and grunted. "Oh, my hand. You want to cripple me for good?" He made a great show out of shaking his hand and blowing his palm; but when Kyler watched with the patience of an old man, Pete had to work hard to hide his disappointment.

He tossed an easy throw to the boy and, when he caught it, called, "Come on, Kyler. Make her work for it." But Kyler's throw was so weak Laureen had to race forward to catch it.

After a few minutes of trying to get some sort of enthusiasm out of the boy, Pete gave up and put the ball in the truck.

He pulled Laureen to his side and took Kyler's hand. "Maybe we'll enjoy the swings more."

Laureen pulled Kyler up on one swing and plopped on the one next to him. "You think Pete can push us both?"

Kyler nodded, as solemn as a funeral director.

Pete laughed. "You might have to take turns." He gave Laureen's swing a big push that sent her high into the air then raced over to give Kyler a push. He raced back to Laureen then hurried back to Kyler, tickling him as the swing arced back.

Kyler squirmed and made a small sound, more a grunt than a giggle, but it was reward enough.

If only he would open up.

As if afraid of the wee bit he'd let himself go, he skidded to a stop and got off the swing. His back rigid, he walked slowly away.

Laureen and Pete followed.

"It's like he's afraid to let himself have fun," Pete said.

"I suppose he is. He never lets himself have fun with people he doesn't feel comfortable with. He had just begun to relax around Frank and Ann. He even took his wooden man with him and told them how he had made it. It was a big step for him." She laid her head against his shoulder as they walked. He knew she ached over Kyler's regression.

"Then just when he's deciding to trust—wham!—he gets hit in the face by their rejection."

"Any chance they'll change their minds?"

"I don't think so."

Kyler led them to the duck pond. The boy sat on the grassy edge and watched the birds paddling around on the pond.

Pete and Laureen exchanged glances and then sat beside him—Pete on one side, Laureen on the other. They held him close in a three-cornered hug.

A slow, desperate ache engulfed Pete. He'd give anything to be able to help Kyler. And ease Laureen's distress over this turn of events.

ಸಿ

Laureen had spent every spare moment with Kyler, talking to him as she had before, but as the days passed he seemed more withdrawn than ever.

In the third week, the administration for Barnabas Christian Home called a meeting to plan a direction for Kyler's care.

Laureen attended. But she was unprepared for the decision.

"The psychologist feels Kyler has regressed so far that he needs much more specialized, intensive help," she was told. "We've arranged to move him to the residential home staffed to deal with his sort of problem."

Laureen faced the assembled group around the table. They were sympathetic and regretful, and she knew they were wrong. She pushed to her feet. "I've worked with him for two years now. I've had encouraging success. I feel a move to unfamiliar people and routine will undo all I've gained."

"He's gone backward," the head supervisor said.

"He's had a terrible disappointment."

"Yes. It's unfortunate. But we can't undo it. Or deny the damage it's done."

"Moving him will do more damage," she insisted.

"Our joint opinion is it will open up another opportunity for him."

Laureen stood facing them feeling as if she'd been wrapped in tight ropes. Unless she could offer a better alternative Kyler would be moved, ripping a huge permanent hole in her heart. She loved the boy even as she knew he loved her. In fact, she and Pete were probably the only ones he'd allowed himself to love since his mother's death.

One of the supervisors gave her a sorrowful look. "We all agree that what Kyler needs is a permanent home with people who love him, but that doesn't seem about to happen. We have to make some hard choices here."

Laureen's gaze circled the table slowly. They all agreed. She alone was the dissenting voice. A core of resolve stiffened her spine. She would continue to defend this little boy. She'd do whatever she could to help him.

"We'll adopt him," she said.

twelve

Ten voices spoke at once. Then a hundred questions were thrown at her.

"First," Laureen said, "I need to discuss it with my future husband."

It was the right thing to do. There was not a doubt in her mind.

But what would Pete say?

At one time he'd insisted he wouldn't take such a child into his home, but this wasn't any child. This was Kyler. Pete knew and loved him. It would be okay.

She hurried from the meeting, anxious to talk to him.

As soon as the kitchen was cleaned after the evening meal, she prepared to go next door.

The shop door was open, and Laureen stepped inside. Pete hadn't noticed her entry, allowing her a few minutes to study him unobserved. Curls of wood fell off the bird he carved. His brown hair caught the slanting rays of sun. He looked sober and serious as he focused on his work. The groove in his cheek deepened, and she knew he smiled at some pleasing thought. She hoped it was of her.

He was so strong and steady. He would always be there for her. Never changing, no matter what big or little thing upset her. How she loved him. Together they would provide Kyler with a home where he would find the security he needed.

She must have sighed her happiness for he glanced in her

direction. When he saw her, a slow smile lifted the corners of his mouth. He didn't say anything, just looked at her in that steady way of his.

"I was thinking about you," he said.

The soft tremor of his voice warmed her. "I hope that's what brought the little smile."

"Was I smiling?"

She nodded.

He put aside his carving knife and carefully dusted traces of sawdust from his pants as he stood. When he held out his arms, she hurried into his embrace, pressing her cheek to his chest to feel the reassuring beat of his heart beneath her ear. She wrapped her arms around him and held him so tight he grunted.

She eased the pressure a bit then turned her face upward to receive his sweet kiss full of promises for the future, full of assurances of forever.

"Umm, you taste good," he murmured.

She giggled. "We had chili for supper."

"Not that kind of good."

Without releasing her he drew her to a wooden bench in the corner of the shop.

"How did the meeting go?"

"They had decided to place him in a treatment center."

She felt him start. "You mean move him?"

"Yes. They thought it was the best solution to his problems."

"I hope you talked them out of it."

She gave a muted sound of amusement. "I certainly did." After a pause she added, "They all agreed the best thing for him would be adoption."

"Well, that's a no-brainer."

"I knew you'd agree. If they were to go ahead with this

plan, he'll be headed down a one-way street that will destroy him. First the treatment center, then a group home, then a series of foster homes. It's just not right to subject Kyler to such a fate."

Pete shook his head. "There has to be an alternative."

"There is." She smiled, certain he would see the possibility himself, given a few more minutes. But she couldn't wait for him to come to the conclusion on his own.

"What?" His frown informed her he didn't understand.

"We can adopt him."

He looked as if she'd hit him in the stomach. It was not the reaction she'd expected. He pulled his hand from her shoulder and crossed his arms over his chest.

A shiver snaked up her spine.

"What did you say?" he asked.

"I said we could adopt him," she repeated in a less certain voice. "Pete, he's going to get lost in the system. He'll end up a statistic."

He shook his head. "No, we can't. I told you how I feel about adopting older, problem-ridden children."

She nodded, misery dragging at every pore. "I know, but this isn't some kid. This is Kyler."

"I know who you mean."

"You love Kyler. Doesn't that make a difference?"

The stubborn look on his face sent her emotions spiraling into a dark pit. "This is about you and me." He jerked to his feet. "How could you even suggest it?"

"I"—she swallowed hard—"I guess I thought you loved him."

His dark scowl made her shrink against the hard back of the bench. "I thought I made it plain from the beginning. Troubled kids are too hard on a marriage. And ours will be just starting out."

She pressed her teeth together to keep her jaw from quivering. A deep breath helped her find the strength to face him squarely. "I know you love him. Doesn't that mean anything?"

"Of course it means something. It means I wish him all the best in the future. I'll pray for him."

"But you won't adopt him?"

"Laureen, what we have is too precious to toy with."

"But imagine what will happen to him."

"You're not responsible for every kid that needs a home."

She pushed to her feet, disappointment making her angry. "No, but I'm willing to put my money where my mouth is. I love him enough to do more than think about him. Or pray about him. I care enough to do something."

His chest rose and fell heavily. "Like what?"

"I will adopt him myself." She clenched her hands at her side, silently challenging him to change his mind.

"Laureen, you're not thinking. You and I have something—"

She interrupted. "I will not turn my back on him." She met his gaze defiantly. "Don't make me choose."

"It sounds as if you already have."

Her anger fled. "No, Pete, this is your choice, not mine. I had hoped our love was strong enough to take some risks, if that's how you see Kyler. I don't see him that way. I see him as a little boy I love. I see how he needs to be loved. I see what I *can* do and that is put arms and legs on my love."

"Then I'm afraid there is no chance for us."

She lifted her chin, determined not to let him see how much he had hurt her. "I hope you'll reconsider."

"Laureen." His voice broke. "Don't do this."

Her teeth chattered as she spoke. "If you mean Kyler, I am going to do it. If you mean us. . ." She waited, her throat clogged with tears.

He groaned. "Don't throw away what we have."

"You leave me no choice." Her whisper came straight from her broken heart.

She hurried home, pausing to tell Marj she needed some time alone, and rushed to her room. She managed to hold back her tears until she threw herself on her bed, and then her emotions broke free in a mighty flood.

Later, her scalding tears spent, she picked up her Bible and sat in her armchair. Could she survive this? Not without supernatural help, she knew. "If God does not rescue me, I shall perish," she whispered.

Drawn to the Psalms, she read verse after verse, finding comfort and strength.

Sometime later a knock sounded. In answer to her invitation to enter, Marj stepped into the room.

"Are you okay?" she asked.

"I don't know." Her voice breaking several times, Laureen explained Pete's adamant refusal to agree to the adoption. "I guess I read him wrong," she whispered.

Marj sat on the arm of the chair and hugged her. "I've seen the bond between you and Kyler. It's something special and precious."

Laureen nodded.

"But you have to think this through carefully." Marj paused as if considering her words. "Are you sure you want to adopt as a single mother? Will you be able to work to support the two of you and yet provide the time and care he needs? Where will you get the emotional support you need? And, most of all, are you certain you want to give up Pete and your hopes for marriage and a family of your own?"

Laureen didn't answer. Marj was right. She had many practical matters to consider. "Maybe Pete's not the man I thought he was." Even as she said it, her heart threatened to bleed to death. He was everything she wanted. Or dreamed of. Kind, gentle, steady. But totally unreasonable and unbending.

"Please don't say anything to the kids until I have time to sort out a few things."

Marj readily agreed.

Laureen slept little that night as she put her questions and concerns before the Lord, determined she wouldn't move forward one step until she had full assurance she was doing the right thing.

Toward morning she read a verse that stood out as if it had been written in neon lights. James 1:27 stated, "Religion that God our Father accepts as pure and faultless is this: to look after orphans and widows in their distress."

It was the go-ahead she sought. She knew her decision was the right one. She couldn't help all the widows and orphans, but there was one little orphan she could help.

She rose, put away her Bible and prepared for the day, determined never to glance over her shoulder at what she'd given up.

あ

Working out the details for Kyler's adoption had been easier than she anticipated. No one raised an objection to her adopting as a single mom as long as she could provide for him financially. She began to make plans that no longer included Pete. A big part of her heart was empty and black. She'd never before felt so alone.

Determined not to let it get her down, she poured herself into preparations.

The first thing she'd done was tell Kyler. Marj had taken the other two boys so she could be alone with him. She'd considered not mentioning that Pete would not be part of the adoption, but she knew she had to be honest with Kyler.

She pulled him to her knee to explain what his future held. "Kyler, you know I love you very much, don't you?"

His eyes wary, he nodded.

"In fact, I love you so much I want to be your mommy, your forever mommy."

He watched her. If he felt anything, he refused to show it. But that didn't bother her. She'd seen him open up before and knew he would again given love and time and all sorts of help.

"I am going to adopt you. We'll have a home of our own and be a real family."

She watched him process the information, and then she hugged him close. For a while she held him, rocking him in her arms as she talked about what it would be like. Then she sat him up. "There's one thing, though. Pete and I have decided not to get married, so he won't be adopting you, too."

His eyes widened. They shone with tears. He swallowed very hard then lay against her and let her rub his back. She marveled at this child's strength in the face of one emotional disappointment after another. As she held him, she prayed for strength and wisdom to give him the security he needed.

જ

Pete wasn't surprised that Marj brought Kyler over to work on his project.

He was grateful the figures were almost finished so he could soon ignore the home and its activities and occupants. He bent over the boy to show him a spot that needed sanding.

Kyler shrank back. It wasn't anything big and loud. Just enough withdrawal to ensure that Pete's arm didn't brush Kyler's shoulder. Pete had to admit it hurt a little. But what did he expect? No doubt Laureen had informed him of her plans—and Pete's absence from them. He could hardly expect Kyler's approval.

But he knew he was right.

He prayed Frank and Ann would change their minds, or knowing how strongly Laureen felt about the kids' going to relatives he prayed for some cousins or an aunt or uncle to crawl from the woodwork, asking to be allowed to adopt Kyler.

The day Kyler completed the carving, Pete decided to take the boy back to the home rather than have Marj come over for him. His excuse to himself was he wanted to show Laureen what a good job the boy had done. But he couldn't deny the real reason for his visit—he hoped Laureen had come to her senses.

Laureen opened the door before he knocked. She gave him a guarded look before she bent to Kyler's level.

"You're all finished." She took the three figures and examined them. "What a good job." She straightened and faced Pete. "Tell Pete thank you."

It stung that Kyler huddled against Laureen's legs and refused to look at him as he nodded. Pete knew it was the only thanks the boy would send his way.

Laureen patted Kyler's shoulder. "Put the figures on the table and go find Marj," she said. "She's downstairs playing table tennis with Michael and Davey."

Kyler slipped away as quietly as a shadow.

"He can't say thanks, so I'll say it for him. And I thank you, too, for devoting so much time to helping him."

He nodded. "I hoped we could talk a bit." He wished she would look at him as she had not so long ago, with her eyes brimming with love. Instead she pressed her lips together and opened the door for him to step inside.

"Can I offer you some coffee or something?"

He didn't want anything to eat or drink, but maybe it would help her relax if she had something to do so he said coffee would be nice.

She hurried about filling the pot, putting coffee in the filter, and studiously avoiding looking at him.

Finally she sat down, gripping the warm mug as if needing the extra heat.

Suddenly he was unable to find the words that tangled in his mind every night and all day. Protesting words, demanding their love be salvaged. Aching words of longing and missing. "I want to ask you to reconsider."

"If you mean change my mind about adopting Kyler, I can't." The misery in her blue eyes clawed at his soul.

"Laureen, I know how strongly you feel about your commitment to children."

"You know, but you don't understand."

"How can I? I see things from the exact opposite of the picture." He held up his hands to stop her from speaking. "I wish I could change my mind. I even phoned my cousins and talked to them about what it was like. To see if I was remembering things wrong." His voice dropped to a low rumble. "I hoped I was mistaken, but their story only makes me more sure of my stand. They said Billy was just a regular sort of kid to begin with. He got into a lot of mischief and wasn't very obedient. They said it was really hard on their mom. She had to struggle with him every day while Uncle Norman was at work."

She stared at him, her lips set in a tight line, and it hit him that she looked as if nothing he said would make her change her mind.

He rushed on, determined to make her see and accept the facts. "Bob said as Billy approached adolescence he got worse. He stole things; he wrecked things. Things he thought someone else might value. He grew angrier and more violent. Bob said his dad refused to see it. Or preferred to think it was just a passing phase. When my aunt discovered him in Carol's bed trying to force her to play his girlfriend, my aunt took Carol and Bob and moved out."

Laureen's eyes were cold. "Kyler would never be like that."

"Can you guarantee it?"

"Life doesn't come with guarantees. It comes with many challenges."

Pete shook his head. "I don't want to wonder if he might turn on you someday. I don't want to worry over the safety of children we might have."

"So we're back at square one."

He studied the way her jaw muscles tightened, the ice-cold blue of her eyes. He had never seen her look so stubborn. "Why are you being so close-minded about this? Are you sure it isn't guilt driving you?"

Her fingers stopped twirling her cup. "How can you even say that?"

"You can't deny you've always felt guilty you weren't able to keep your promise to Gina. Laureen, it wasn't your promise to keep."

"I know that. I haven't devoted my life to atoning for that promise, if that's what you think. But I saw the damage of broken promises. I continue to see it. Adults say things to children then revoke their promises with their so-called reasonable excuses."

He lifted his hands. "I want you to change your mind. I love you, Laureen. I don't want to think about living the rest of my life without you."

thirteen

When her lips quivered, he allowed himself to hope.

"This isn't about guilt," she whispered. "It's about love. My love for one innocent little boy who doesn't deserve the horrible things that have come into his life."

"What about our love?" His voice cracked with emotion. "Doesn't our love count for anything?"

Her eyes glistened. The sight of those unshed tears deepened the ache within him. How he longed to hold her and comfort her. Forever and always. But he couldn't with this thing separating them.

"I love you more than you'll ever guess," she said. "I will cherish the little time we've been together for the rest of my life, and I pray the memories will be enough to sustain me." She stood to her feet. Her voice strong and full of resolve, she gave him a look that glowed with purpose. "But do not ask me to choose between you and Kyler. It is not a choice I can make."

Pete lurched to his feet. Without a backward look he hurried blindly from the house. He thought he heard the words, "Good-bye, my love." But he wasn't sure if Laureen spoke them or his heart cried the words silently.

≈

Pete glanced at the calendar over his workbench for the ten thousandth time in the space of two hours. As if he needed the calendar to remind him what day it was. He glanced at his watch and pursed his lips. He vowed he would not look at it again, but five minutes later his gaze returned to his wrist.

He threw down the hammer he'd been holding idly. He couldn't even remember what he planned to do with it.

By now the fair entries would have been judged. He wondered how Kyler had done.

Giving up any pretense of doing work, he put the tools away and locked the shop. The fair was the biggest event of the summer in Freetown, and he didn't intend to miss it just because he might run into someone from the home.

He paid the admission price and wandered through the gates, passing the amusement rides on the way to the arena where the bench show was now open for viewing.

A flash of light caught the dark hair of a woman watching the merry-go-round.

Would he never see dark hair glistening in the sun without having a jolt of regret?

The woman turned, and blue eyes caught the bright sun.

It was Laureen.

Someone could have stabbed holes in his lungs for all the air he could get in.

She turned and saw him. Even across the distance separating them he saw her jerk and look around wildly.

Before she could escape, before he could change his mind, he strode toward her, never letting his gaze leave her eyes. Deep blue wariness.

What had happened to the understanding that drew them together like a magnet a short time ago?

How could they have let it go?

There had to be some way of solving this problem keeping them apart.

But the firm set of her jaw told him she would resist any more arguments from him.

He stopped inches from her, his arms hungry for the feel of her.

But he had to settle for leaning back on his heels and watching her. "I had to come and see how Kyler's entry did."

She seemed relieved at his choice of conversation. "He won first prize. He is so excited."

"Where is he?"

"He took Marj to see his ribbon. He insisted I wait for him here." She glowed with her news.

Pete knew what a big step it was for Kyler to want to go somewhere without Laureen. He wondered if the boy had started talking again but knew he didn't have the right to ask.

"I am so glad for him." He wanted to hold the moment forever. If only there was some way to keep her at his side.

There was. The answer seared through his brain. All he had to do was agree to the adoption.

But he thought of Uncle Norman and how much pain the family had endured and continued to endure, and he could not change his mind.

"We ought to celebrate his victory," he said.

She hesitated. For a tortured moment he thought she would refuse; then she nodded. "What did you have in mind?"

He practically choked. What he had in mind was grabbing her in his arms and running away with her. Running until she forgot about Kyler. Running so far only he and Laureen existed.

He took a deep breath and looked around. "How about a ride?"

She nodded, rather reluctantly, he thought.

The Ferris wheel was the closest ride, and he led her in that direction before she could change her mind.

❧

Laureen allowed Pete to lead her to the amusement ride. She slipped to the wooden seat, making room for him beside her.

Her brain had stopped functioning. She wanted so much for him to pull her into his arms and say he'd changed his mind. Every cell in her body ached for him. Nothing mattered but his voice, his touch, his words.

No. She clung to a shred of reason. Kyler mattered more than anything else in her life. More than life itself.

The steel vise of duty and love held her steady despite her trembling emotions.

The attendant slid the steel bar across in front of them and snapped it into place. The seat swung and jerked as they inched ahead.

"How have things been going?" Pete asked.

She faced him. Did he mean generally or regarding the adoption? "I've been busy. There are three interviews booked for next week."

"Your potential replacement?"

"Yes. And I've been considering where or what I should do for a job."

"I thought you planned to stay on at the home—working the day shift."

"I want to be home with Kyler when he gets back from school. That conflicts with when I'd be needed at the home." The ride jerked forward, again and again, each stop and start setting their bench swinging. Laureen held the restraining bar and paid little attention. Her focus was on Pete. She studied every feature of his face, knowing she would never forget a single detail but wanting to store up as many mental pictures of him as she could. She studied the shape of his finely arched brows, the way his skin had darkened over the summer, the way his hair dipped over his forehead.

He studied her every bit as closely, as desperately as she studied him.

She had a feeling of impending disaster. They were making the biggest mistake of their lives. Somehow she had to convince him to change his mind. She had to make him see that taking Kyler was the right thing for them to do together.

She looked away so she could think and gasped. The ground lay far below them; the people looked like little game pieces on a Monopoly board. The seat rocked back and forth. What was she doing on a Ferris wheel? Her mouth dried to the texture of sandpaper. Nausea twisted her stomach. She squeezed the bar until her knuckle popped. She closed her eyes and moaned.

"Laureen?" Pete's voice sounded a long way off. He touched her shoulder. She shuddered. When he wrapped his arms around her, she managed to unlatch her fingers from the bar and bury her face in his chest, clinging to him until she wondered if he could still breathe.

"I'm sorry," he crooned. "I totally forgot about your fear of heights. I'll hold you until we're down. You'll be okay. I'd never let anything happen to you."

Keeping her fingers curled into the material of his shirt for security, she twisted enough to allow herself to lift her face to him. He accepted her unspoken request and kissed her.

They swung to a stop. As soon as the attendant threw the bar back, Pete grabbed her hand and, running, took her to a quiet spot behind one of the tents.

"Look," he said, his voice deep with urgency. "What we have is too precious to throw away."

He'd changed his mind. Her prayers had been answered. The skin around Laureen's eyes felt smoother, softer than it had for weeks. "I'm glad you finally see it."

He traced the line of her jaw, his gaze following the trail of his finger.

"Kyler won't be a risk to our marriage," she said, her lips quivering. "He'll be part of the glue that keeps us together."

He dropped his hands to his side and straightened. "I meant you and me. What we have."

Cold hard steel drove through her heart. "I love you, Pete Long. Even if you are so dense you make pudding look clear. But unless your love for me includes Kyler, your love is too small."

They stared at each other. Laureen was sure the resolve she felt showed on her face, even as Pete's resolve showed on his. She would give anything if they could change the way things were between them.

"Mommy." The sound of Kyler's voice reached her and strengthened her decision.

Kyler still didn't say a lot, but she felt certain that one word would never fail to thrill her.

"Hi, sweetie." She bent to catch him as he hurtled himself into her arms. "Pete has come to congratulate you on winning first prize." She felt the child stiffen, and she hugged him tighter. The hurt Pete's defection had inflicted on Kyler's life was perhaps the greatest pain of all.

"I knew you would do well," Pete said. He bent low to face the child. "You are a real good woodworker. I'm willing to bet that someday you'll be famous for your carvings."

Laureen's fingers pinched together in Kyler's tight grip as the child faced Pete. She knew he wouldn't talk. He had put on that stoic look she knew so well. He wouldn't have anything more to say than one of his wooden figures.

Pete knew it, too, and straightened, pain flashing across his face before he leaned back on his heels.

She wished she could end this triangle of pain. Everyone feeling lost and disillusioned. But she couldn't do anything. Pete was the only one with the power to turn things around. But Pete was a stubborn man with his own powerful, but misguided, reasons.

"I'm going to have a look at them now," Pete said. He waited a moment. Laureen felt sorry for him. Did he realize how much he was willing to sacrifice because of his uncle's bad experience?

She prayed for God to help him see the mistake he was making and then took pity on the man. "Kyler and I will show you where his entry is." Marj waved at them and turned to go in the other direction.

Kyler clung to her hand as they headed back to the arena.

Laureen wondered if she had made a mistake in offering to go with Pete. Every step of the way she ached for the distance between them to be bridged. She felt his every breath as if it were her own.

A noisy bunch of kids rushed past them, forcing her to side-step to avoid being run over. She brushed into Pete. When he reached out a hand to steady her, she fought a weakness that threatened to steal away her resolve.

Kyler's hand in hers, holding on as if he thought she'd disappear into the crowd, anchored her. Slowly she brought her swirling emotions into submission.

She loved Pete. She always would. But as she'd told him he was dense. Blind to the possibilities of the future. All he saw, all he'd let himself see, was the disaster of his uncle's experience.

She stepped from his side and stayed several inches away as she led him to the exhibit.

❧

Pete paced the kitchen floor in his house. He should never have gone to the fair. Everything he had gained over the past weeks had been undone by that visit.

Not the visit, he corrected himself, the kiss. He had acted the fool kissing her. Allowing himself false hope. He resolved afresh to avoid everyone and everything to do with the home. Even as he made the promise, he knew he could never keep his thoughts from flying next door or his heart from remembering the feel of Laureen in his arms nor her lips on his. And certainly he would never forget the way she slid into his emotions with the power to make everything else pale in comparison.

He slammed out the door. The lawn had been mowed twice already this week, but he planned to mow it again. At this rate he'd have the best manicured lawn in the whole town.

He pulled the mower out of the shop and wiped it clean with a rag. He snorted. He had the cleanest lawnmower in the whole country, too.

From the first moment he'd felt himself attracted to Laureen, he suspected he'd come in second best if she ever had to choose between him and one of the kids. It wasn't as if she hadn't warned him.

Having seen the heartbreak and agony of adopting an older child, he knew love wasn't enough to guarantee a happily-ever-after ending.

He should have never let himself fall in love with her.

A muffled voice carried on the warm summer air. He stood up and listened carefully, thinking he heard his name.

Now your imagination is really getting out of control, he chided himself. *Next thing you'll be seeing Laureen under every overhanging branch.*

But he was sure he'd heard his name.

He'd promised himself to stay as far away from the yard next door as possible, but he couldn't help himself. He eased over to the fence and peeked over.

Kyler sat alone in the sandbox. At first Pete couldn't see what he played with; then Kyler held something over his head. It was one of the wooden figures he'd carved.

The boy shifted, allowing Pete a better view. The child plunked the figure into the corner of the sandbox. As he played, Kyler mumbled.

Pete strained to catch what he said.

"You come back," Kyler ordered and grabbed the man figure. He shoved him in the sand beside the child and woman figures standing together. He picked up the child figure. "Look, Mommy. Pete's here. He did come."

He picked up the woman figure and spoke in a high voice. "Kyler, you are so smart."

Then he lined up the three figures again, the man on one side of the child, the woman on the other.

"Pete, Kyler, Mommy," he whispered.

Anger such as he had never felt in his life blasted through Pete. Of all the low-down, stinking tricks. This one beat all.

fourteen

He knew Laureen would do everything in her power to make him change his mind. But setting up the boy? That was despicable. Something he wouldn't have expected from her.

He'd put a double-quick stop to this nonsense.

He marched out his back gate and threw open the rattling gate next door. Without pausing to look at Kyler, yet sensing the boy's alarm, he strode to the back door and banged on it hard enough to scrape his knuckles.

Laureen opened the door, her eyes widening at the look on his face. He held his breath for a minute to calm his anger. "You and I have to talk." He stormed inside without waiting for an invitation.

"Do come in," she muttered. "Make yourself right at home," she added, as he jerked back a chair and planted himself in it. "To what do I owe this honor?"

He ignored the sarcasm in her voice. "I never thought I'd see you stoop so low." The room rang with his low anger-controlled words.

She glanced at her feet as if wondering what she'd done.

"Don't play innocent with me."

She gave him a cold look as she sat across the table from him. "I have no idea what you are talking about."

"You make promises you can't back away from. Then on top of that you make promises to the boy you can't keep."

She interrupted. "Any promise I make to Kyler I intend to keep."

"And then you set him up to try to manipulate me into going along with this promise-keeping of yours. I will not be pushed into something I know won't end up as wonderful as you'd like to believe."

She leaned back in her chair, her hands hugging her shoulders. He ignored her defensive posture.

Her eyes bleak, she said, "I have no idea what you are talking about."

He slid forward to the edge of his chair. "You can make all the promises you want to Kyler. That's your business. But when you promise him things that involve me, then you better get my permission first."

She shook her head back and forth. "I think it's time you explained yourself."

"As if you don't know. How dare you promise him I'll be joining you!"

"I what?"

"I overheard him in the sandbox. It's obvious he thinks I'm part of this"—he waved a hand—"this adoption."

Her breath came out in a gust. "I see. And you think I told him this?"

"Are you going to deny it?"

"There doesn't seem to be much point. You've already made up your mind."

The anger fled as quickly as it came. "Okay, maybe I was hasty." He ignored her unladylike snort. "But if you didn't tell him that, who did?"

"What makes you think anyone did?"

He sat very still. "Where would he get the idea then?"

"He's a little boy with a head full of wants and dreams. Did it ever cross your stubborn mind this might be his dream?"

He could think of nothing to say.

She pressed her lips together tightly.

He wished he could say or do something to ease the pain darkening her eyes. But they had reached an impasse. Neither of them could or would change. They had found an ideological difference that was unsolvable. He knew he should be grateful they discovered this vast unbridgeable gulf before they married. But he was not. He resented the timing, the circumstances. Everything.

She sighed. "Poor Kyler. A little boy with big dreams. It's not fair he should have his dreams dashed to pieces time after time."

What could he say? If she'd meant for her words to condemn him she had succeeded. But what alternative did he have? Laureen wanted Kyler more than she wanted him.

And he wanted a normal, destined-to-succeed marriage.

"I can't help wondering what your attitude would have been if Kyler were my biological child." Her agonized tone ripped through his heart. "Would you still expect me to choose between the two of you?"

"That's hardly the same thing. This isn't your child."

"If you mean he isn't bone of my bone and flesh of my flesh, you are correct. But if you mean he isn't one hundred per cent born in my heart, you couldn't be more wrong." She shivered, but he sensed her resolve deepening. "I have never physically carried a child beneath my heart for nine months, so I can't say I know what it's like. But I have carried Kyler in my heart for over two years. I loved him the first time he looked at me with a depth of feeling in those beautiful eyes of his, and I felt a connection so deep and profound in my heart that I can truthfully say it turned me practically inside out."

"Laureen, this is your job. You must have seen dozens of kids come and go. Did you want to rescue each one of them and take them home for your own?"

A slow smile softened her features. "I know all about being able to detach emotionally. We were taught how to give everything yet not give away anything of ourselves. I've mourned the going of several of the kids because I was so fond of them or because I knew the future held more sorrow for them. But"—she sat up straight and fixed him with such a piercing gaze he almost flinched—"I can honestly say I have never bonded like this with another child. I love Kyler with a love that will not let him go. I love him enough to make profound sacrifices."

He knew she meant him. She would let him go before she would ever let something come between her and Kyler.

He had only one more defense. "I have been praying Frank and Ann would change their minds and come back for him. I've been praying you would come to your senses and see you aren't the only solution for Kyler. Something else will come up. Just wait."

"You have been praying the wrong prayer." Her conviction stung. How could she tell him what was right for him to pray? "Why don't you pray for the courage to love one little boy?"

He strode from the room before he said something he would regret. Never in his life had he met a more stubborn, headstrong, blind woman. He should be thankful he had discovered this flaw in her before they married.

He told himself so all the way home and all the next day. He would keep telling himself until he believed it.

❧

Laureen continued with plans.

She interviewed applicants and, along with the administration, chose her successor.

She decided to move back home and rented a house a block from her parents. Her brother, Stuart, lived two blocks away in the other direction. She'd spent hours discussing the adoption with her family, making it clear she wanted lots of family involvement.

"I want Kyler to be surrounded by people who love him and are willing to invest themselves in his life."

Her parents, her brothers, and their wives were eager to provide lots of support to Kyler.

"But we'll be here for you, too," Mom said. "And we don't want you to forget it. You'll never be on your own in raising Kyler."

She could hardly wait for the day she took him to their new home.

She pushed aside the feeling of loneliness that haunted her late at night. She and Pete were not meant to be. She'd prayed for God's will. And now she prayed for grace to accept it.

She'd taken a temporary job as a consultant for the local school board—a job that would allow her to be home when Kyler returned from school. She wanted to devote herself to him.

Michael and Davey were moving to the back country to join their mother and stepfather. Laureen had talked extensively to them, preparing them for the move. She knew they faced many challenges in this placement, but she hoped and prayed it would work out.

All she had left to do was wait for the new staff members

to take their place. Everything was set for the last weekend before school started.

Her furniture had been hauled away and placed in her new home by her brother and father. Tomorrow she'd load the car with the last of the things she and Kyler were taking with them, and they would be on their way.

She had one more thing she wanted to do. Even though it hurt just to think of it, she wanted to say a last good-bye to Pete.

She waited for half an hour after he returned home. Then she knew if she waited any longer she would chicken out.

Checking her hair in the mirror and giving it another brushing, she asked Marj to watch the boys while she was gone.

Feeling as if she might shatter at any moment, she forced her steps down the path, along the few yards of alley. She paused, took a deep breath, and stepped into Pete's backyard.

He sat in a lawn chair watching her.

Her heart raced into a frenzy; yet her limbs were cold and limp. Her feet felt as if they were buried in cement. How could she say good-bye to the man she loved?

"Can I offer you a soda?" he asked, his voice sounding distant and tinny in her ears. It wasn't his voice, she knew; it was the echo of her own pain.

"No, I won't be long."

She collapsed on the chair he nodded toward, surprised her legs had held her up that long. "We're leaving tomorrow. I've come to say good-bye."

At first he didn't speak, just rested his soda can on his knee and stared at the side of the shop. Then he grunted. "I thought you'd be staying on at the home."

"No. I've decided to go back home." She told him her plans.

"Umm. Sounds like everything has worked out just fine."

"Almost everything," she whispered.

"I guess this is really good-bye then."

"I guess so." *Unless you give me some reason to think you've changed your mind. Or that you're reconsidering.*

But he sat as unmovable as a slab of pine.

She rose unsteadily to her feet. "We're leaving in the morning."

He knew their timetable. If he intended to change his mind, he had better hurry up or she'd be gone.

Somehow she made it back to the home. Sometime during the evening feeling returned to her heart. She was sorry it did.

It was really over. She'd hoped right to the end things would work out. Now she had to accept the inevitable.

God, be my strength and guide. Without You I will come undone.

Slowly, surely, strength and resolve returned.

She wasn't the first woman to face raising a child on her own. Nor was she the first one to face losing the love of her life. God was sufficient for her needs.

She knew she would learn to lean on her faith in a deeper way in the future.

❧

Pete wished he could be anywhere but home watching Laureen carry the last of her things out to her car. Too bad it was a Saturday and the plumbing shop was closed.

He hid in his shop, trying to force himself to work on his carving, but it only reminded him of the times Laureen had brought Kyler over.

Would he ever be able to enter this building again without sensing her presence?

He would finish renovating the house, sell it, and move as soon as possible.

Maybe he'd set up a new business—renovating older homes. He began to feel better thinking of a business he knew he would enjoy more than he did plumbing. He could leave the plumbing business under the management of his shop foreman.

He knew he would never forget Laureen. She was the sun and moon of his heart.

He bowed his head over his hands. *God, why did You let me fall in love with her? Why did You bring her into my life?*

What did God expect Christians to do with kids like Kyler? Certainly provide care for them. He knew homes such as the Barney House were necessary.

But adoption?

His thoughts were interrupted by the sound of a door slamming.

Michael called to someone—probably Davey. *Okay, admit it, mister. You'll miss those kids.*

Especially Kyler.

That little kid was really something. He hoped he'd hear how he was doing in the future.

Had they finished packing and left yet?

One more glimpse was all he wanted. He pushed the wood and tools away and hurried outside, afraid they had already driven away.

But Laureen's car was still there, the trunk lid in the air. He couldn't imagine what more she planned to cram in. It looked as if there wasn't room for an envelope.

Then he saw Kyler sitting in the passenger seat, waiting, and looking toward Pete's house. A look of such longing and pain creased the boy's face that Pete half reached out his hand to—to do what? he wondered. He had already mentally severed himself from the child. Why was he torturing himself like this?

Kyler held up the three wooden figures Pete had helped him carve.

He'd miss the kid. He'd wormed his way into Pete's heart and wasn't about to vacate it. Pete swallowed hard. Something had to be caught in the back of his throat.

Laureen stepped to the sidewalk with a bag of papers and stowed them in the trunk then slammed the lid.

Pete ducked back, not wanting her to see him gawking at her like a starved tramp staring at a banquet.

She climbed in behind the wheel, hooked her seat belt, and checked Kyler's.

The motor started. Laureen reached over the back of the seat as if looking for something.

Kyler's face remained pressed against the glass, the wooden figures crowded at the side of his head.

Drive away, Pete silently begged. *Go now before I fall apart on the sidewalk.* But Laureen still dug among the piles of stuff in the back seat.

Kyler's lips moved. He was trying to tell Pete something. He mouthed the words again.

It looked like—no, it couldn't be.

Pete was certain the boy said, "I love you."

He loved him!

It had never crossed his mind the child could love him.

This child, who had known rejection and pain on every side, still had the inner strength to let himself love another adult. An undeserving, unfaithful adult. One who was willing to repeat the pattern of rejection in this kid's life.

· A thousand questions blasted through Pete's brain.

Why could he not bring himself to admit his love for this child?

Because—the answer came, as solid and firm as the ground upon which he stood—because he didn't have the guts to admit he might have been wrong in making a blanket statement about adopting older children.

Because, too, he didn't have the faith to trust God for the future if it included this kid. A God who believed in adoptions. God had been willing to adopt Pete into his family—sins and all.

Suddenly the idea of a future without Kyler doubled his pain at losing Laureen. How could he let this boy and this woman drive away?

Laureen started the motor, glanced over her shoulder to check for traffic, and began to edge away from the curb.

His vision blurred. The whole scene took on a wavy appearance. He brushed at his eyes to clear his vision. Moisture clung to his fingers. He rubbed them together.

He was crying. Pete Long never cried. But the moisture on his hand disproved the fact.

He knew the tears would blur the rest of his life if he didn't stop Kyler and Laureen from walking out of his life.

He lunged after the car, but already Laureen had turned the corner and was headed out of town.

He banged the heel of his hand against his forehead. He'd made the biggest mistake of his life.

He spun around and dashed for his truck. He'd follow her.

But he didn't have an address.

He detoured and headed for the house next door to bang on the door.

Marj opened it.

"What's her address?" he demanded. "I've changed my mind," he added so she'd understand his urgency.

Marj smiled. "I've been praying you'd come to your senses." She plucked a piece of paper off the fridge and handed it to him. "You better take good care of her."

"I will." He hesitated. "If she'll give me another chance."

"You go talk to her."

He was already down the steps and halfway across the yard. He jumped into his truck and spun his wheels leaving the yard. He skidded around the corner and then warned himself to slow down. She'd be there when he got there. No point in taking risks.

He watched for her car along the highway but didn't catch up to her until he reached the address Marj had given him. She must have just arrived because she still sat in the car.

He hurried to her side and knocked on the window.

The look of surprise and joy on her face was something he would remember the rest of his life.

She rolled the window down. "What are you doing here?"

"I just about made the stupidest mistake of my life."

She stared at him then slowly climbed out of the car.

Tears streamed down Pete's face as he pulled her into his arms. "I can't believe I almost let both of you go out of my life." Keeping one arm tightly around her, he hurried to Kyler's door. He had to release her long enough to reach in and get Kyler.

He crushed the boy to his chest. Shifting Kyler to one arm, Pete wrapped his other arm around her and pulled her close, pressing her head to one shoulder as Kyler buried his face against Pete's neck.

"I have been the biggest fool," Pete murmured. "I almost made the most colossal mistake in the world. Laureen, please forgive me for being so stupid. You, too, Kyler."

Kyler nodded, but Laureen waited.

"I thought every situation was the same as my uncle's. I refused to see the truth. I refused to see that Kyler is different. That we're different. That God is sufficient. I never stopped loving you, but I've been blind and stupid and selfish. Can you forgive me?"

"I can't guarantee there won't be problems," Laureen said.

He understood her need to have him clear this up. "I know there will be problems. Everyone has them. As you said, life is full of challenges. But I'm willing to face them. No matter what the future holds, I want to spend my life loving you. Both of you."

Kyler sighed. "I knowed you'd change your mind."

Pete tipped back so he could look into the boy's face. "How did you know?"

Kyler gave him a solemn look. "Because I asked God."

"You are a very wise boy." Pete set the boy on his feet before turning back to Laureen. He dropped to one knee and held her hands between his. "Laureen, will you marry me?"

"Yes, yes, a thousand times, yes." She leaned over and gave him a gentle kiss.

epilogue

Laureen carried baby Jesse into the house. Pete followed, his arms full of flowers and gifts received in the short time she'd been in the hospital. Kyler proudly carried Laureen's overnight bag.

She sat on the couch and looked around her home, her heart overflowing with peace and happiness.

It was great living so close to her parents who had unreservedly poured their love on Kyler. He adored them, and they adored him. And he loved his uncles and aunts and cousins. He had even turned into a chatterbox.

Pete put the flowers in the center of the table and sat beside her, wrapping his arm around her and nuzzling her cheek. "Happy, Mrs. Long?"

"Decidedly."

She looked toward Kyler standing in the doorway. "Come and see your baby brother."

Kyler edged toward them.

Laureen opened the blanket so he could study the baby. She began to wonder at Kyler's quietness.

"Isn't he tiny?" she asked.

Kyler nodded. "Was I that tiny?"

"I expect so. Most babies are pretty little to start with. Do you want to hold him?"

Kyler nodded, his face wrapped in eagerness and awe. He sat beside Pete, and she placed the baby in his arms.

"This is your baby, right?" he asked.

She nodded. "Mine and Pete's and yours."

"So now you're a real family."

Laureen met Pete's glance over Kyler's head. They had discussed this with Kyler many times, how the baby wouldn't change how they felt about him. But faced with the wonder of a new life he still had his doubts.

"Kyler," Pete said. "We've been a real family for a long time. Having another member doesn't change anything except to give us all some more responsibility and lots more reasons to love."

"Jesse is one lucky little boy," Laureen added. "He has a mommy and daddy to love him and take care of him." She stroked Kyler's head. "And he has a big brother who will love him and show him all kinds of big brother things."

Kyler considered her words. "You think he'd like to learn to carve?"

Laureen laughed. "If he doesn't he'll probably like watching his big brother create toys for him."

Kyler looked thoughtful. "But he's your real baby."

Pete patted Kyler's head and shoulders. "You feel pretty real to me, son. I love you, and Mommy loves you. We will never stop loving you."

"Okay. Can I go play now?"

Laureen took the baby from him, and he ran to his room.

She and Pete sat watching Jesse sleep.

Pete sighed.

"Are you okay?" she asked.

He shrugged. "Do you think he'll ever get over me almost letting him go?"

"I think he will always need lots of reassurance of our love."

She pressed her cheek to his shoulder, loving the strength she felt there. "It's like you said—it will give us lots more chances to love him."

She sat quietly, content in the warmth of his love and the gentle breathing of their newborn son. Her joy was complete.

Besides the certainty of Pete's love, she knew one more thing would last forever—God's goodness and His ability to change hearts.

A Letter To Our Readers

Dear Reader:

In order that we might better contribute to your reading enjoyment, we would appreciate your taking a few minutes to respond to the following questions. We welcome your comments and read each form and letter we receive. When completed, please return to the following:

Fiction Editor
Heartsong Presents
PO Box 719
Uhrichsville, Ohio 44683

1. Did you enjoy reading *Forever in My Heart* by Linda Ford?
   ❏ Very much! I would like to see more books by this author!
   ❏ Moderately. I would have enjoyed it more if

   _____

   _____

   _____

2. Are you a member of **Heartsong Presents**? ❏ Yes ❏ No
   If no, where did you purchase this book? _____

   _____

3. How would you rate, on a scale from 1 (poor) to 5 (superior), the cover design? _____

4. On a scale from 1 (poor) to 10 (superior), please rate the following elements.

   ____ Heroine   ____ Plot
   ____ Hero   ____ Inspirational theme
   ____ Setting   ____ Secondary characters

5. These characters were special because?_____

_____

_____

6. How has this book inspired your life?_____

_____

_____

7. What settings would you like to see covered in future
   Heartsong Presents books? _____

_____

_____

8. What are some inspirational themes you would like to see
   treated in future books? _____

_____

_____

9. Would you be interested in reading other **Heartsong
   Presents** titles? ❏ Yes ❏ No

10. Please check your age range:
    ❏ Under 18   ❏ 18-24
    ❏ 25-34   ❏ 35-45
    ❏ 46-55   ❏ Over 55

Name_____

Occupation _____

Address _____

City_____ State_____ Zip_____

HIDDEN MOTIVES

4 stories in 1

Suspense, mystery, and danger pervade the four stories of this romance collection. As love blossoms for four women, threatening situations also arise where hidden motives abound.

Authors Carol Cox of Arizona, Gail Gaymer Martin of Michigan, DiAnn Mills of Texas, and Jill Stengl of Wisconsin, teamed up to create this suspense-filled romance collection.

Contemporary, paperback, 352 pages, 5 ³/₁₆" x 8"

Heart♥ong

Any 12 Heartsong Presents titles for only $27.00*

CONTEMPORARY ROMANCE IS CHEAPER BY THE DOZEN!

Buy any assortment of twelve *Heartsong Presents* titles and save 25% off of the already discounted price of $2.97 each!

*plus $2.00 shipping and handling per order and sales tax where applicable.

HEARTSONG PRESENTS TITLES AVAILABLE NOW:

(If ordering from this page, please remember to include it with the order form.)